Maggie's Magic Chocolate Moon

By Laura Dower

raintree

a Capstone company — publishers for children

Raintree is an imprint of Capstone Global Library Limited, a company incorporated in England and Wales having its registered office at 264 Banbury Road, Oxford, OX2 7DY – Registered company number: 6695582

www.raintree.co.uk
myorders@raintree.co.uk

Edited by Kristen Mohn
Designed by Philippa Jenkins
Original illustrations © 2017 Capstone Global Limited Library
Illustrated by Lilly Lazuli
Production by Kathy McColley
Originated by Capstone Global Limited Library
Printed and bound in China.

ISBN 978 1 4747 2215 5
20 19 18 17 16
10 9 8 7 6 5 4 3 2 1

British Library Cataloguing in Publication Data
A full catalogue record for this book is available from the British Library.

Contents

Talk of the town

Home
Meet the bakers
Recipes
- Cakes
- Cookies
- Tray bakes
- Breads
- Gluten free
- Vegan
- Dairy free
- Other

Archive
- January
- February
- March

Hello, Sweeties!

When we first opened our doors and you came flooding inside, I didn't know what to think. A tidal wave of neighbours is like the world's biggest hug! Thanks to everyone who came out during our first weeks to try our cookies and pies. We're fully up and running now, so we can bake around the clock! Check out our new loaves of bread and my Nana Belle's Can't-Stop-Eating-That-Challah Knots!

And hooray! We have got some reviews for the bakery online and off.

Look at what some of our new friends have to say:

"Daisy's Desserts gets an A+. No, make that a Y. For Yum!" –Neighbourhood Rag

"The west side of town finally gets the bakery wonderland we've all been waiting for. It's a place to consume massive amounts of glaze and chocolate, but it's also a place to sit with an espresso, take in the sights of the neighbourhood and connect with others. Stop in if you have a chance. You won't be disappointed." –Baked Goody Blog

"Have you met the new kid on the block? At the centre of this brand-new neighbourhood bakery is Daisy, the owner and baker, who makes time for each and every customer even as she's rushing to bake more of her hot apple bars which are   BAR NONE!" –Just in Times

And to think, this is only the beginning of our great glazed journey together! What else can possibly be in store? Think pistachios, liquorice and white chocolate (just some of the new and fun flavours I'm playing around with in my kitchen)!

There's plenty of baked love to go around here.

See you inside the cupboard!

xo, Daisy

Sugar free

Maggie McAllister gazed out of her bedroom window from her Nana's house on Sycamore Street. The trees had begun to lose their leaves, and the branches shook gently as the morning breeze blew. Hidden in the top branches of one tree was a large painted bird feeder. Nana had it placed in full view so Maggie and her sister, Grace, could watch the birds gather and feed all winter long. Right now there was a robin poking its beak into the air, ruffling his bright red feathers.

Maggie threw a slipper at the window. It made a thud. The bird flew away.

Often Maggie would find herself staring into space, out of windows and up into the cloudy sky. She did far more staring and thinking than talking. In fact, she hadn't said much for the past several months. Not since the accident. The only person she ever really talked to was Nana or the housekeepers or Grace, of course. Well, she talked to Grace when Grace wasn't being Annoying with a capital *A*. Or when Maggie wasn't feeling Angry with a capital *A*. But Maggie seemed to be angry a lot of the time. And Grace was annoying *all* of the time.

Outside, Maggie could hear the sounds of cars and footsteps, voices of people making their way up and down the street. She slid the window open. A smell of cool autumn air rushed in, and Maggie took big gulps of air. She caught a whiff of something different from usual, though. Different better. Was that food? Maggie's tummy grumbled. Was it coming from the Indian Café? Franco's Italian Galleon? It smelled warm and sweet, like fresh bread.

There was no smell better than fresh bread.

Mum used to bake fresh bread every Sunday. And Dad used to eat it all before Monday even came. That wonderful smell brought back so many memories.

"Mags!" Grace ran into the bedroom with an armful of clothes. "I need your help. Which one?" She held up two T-shirts that looked exactly alike to Maggie.

"Huh?" Maggie sighed with exasperation. "Who cares? It's just school, not a fashion show. Boring, awful, friendless school."

"Come on," Grace said. "You're not friendless." She tilted her head as she looked in the full-length mirror, arranging her perfect brown curls. Maggie's curls were red and wild and impossible to tame.

"Right. Name one friend," Maggie demanded.

"Um," Grace thought hard. "Me?"

Maggie rolled her eyes. "Little sisters don't count."

"I am so glad that Nana said she'd take us shopping this week," Grace said, ignoring Maggie's comment. "I need new shoes and some of that yummy-ummy citrus mint lotion. And trousers, I *definitely* need new trousers."

"You already have a wardrobe full of trousers. And you have enough lotion!" Maggie thought that her sister cared far too much for clothes and "signature scents" for a nine year old.

"No, I don't," Grace pouted.

"Yes, you do!" Maggie insisted.

"Stop bossing me around," said Grace, frowning.

"Why? I'm older and wiser."

"Older maybe, but you're definitely not *wiser*!"" Grace snapped.

"You're such a spoiled little–"

"Takes one to know one," Grace yelled before Maggie could finish her insult. Then Grace threw a pillow at Maggie's head. Unfortunately, it nearly decapitated Moon, the sisters' black cat, named for the white circle between her dainty shoulder blades. She looked like a night sky with one bright spot.

Mum and Dad had adopted Moon when Maggie

was only five and Grace was still in nappies. This cat had been through so much with the girls. Maggie wondered what Moon would say if cats could talk? Did she miss Mum and Dad too?

"*Mwwwwwwwoooow!*" Moon howled.

"Sorry, Moon!" Grace cried. But then she threw another pillow at her sister, this time with better aim. "Take that!" Grace wailed, caught up in the moment, laughing a little.

Maggie was so mad. How could Grace be laughing? Moon darted under the bed to safety. Clever cat.

"Grace, you could have hurt Moon!" Maggie roared. She grabbed the pillow and threw it back at Grace's head – hard.

"*OWWW!*"

Grace wasn't going to let her sister get away with that. She started an all-out pillowfight. The girls went back and forth until one wayward toss from Grace sent Maggie's lamp flying off the bedside table with a smash.

"Look what you did!" Maggie yelled.

"Me?" Grace gasped and burst into tears. "You made me! Astrid! Astrid!" Grace disappeared down the hall to tattle to the nanny (as if Maggie needed one!). In Nana's house, there were people to do every kind of possible task: cooking, laundry, cleaning, gardening and even tutoring. Astrid was in charge of Maggie and Grace whenever Nana was at board meetings or charity auctions or gardening clubs. Which was often.

"Really?" Maggie sighed. "Here we go again." Somehow *she'd* be blamed for this. That was how it usually played out.

Of course Maggie should have been nicer to Grace than she was, especially since they were basically all alone in the world now except for Nana and Moon. But she wasn't. Grace laughed at the dumbest things, and not much was funny to Maggie anymore. It was like Maggie had this black cloud to keep her company. No matter what she did or said, that cloud stayed overhead. Meanwhile, Grace stood in the bright sun and kept right on loving her life.

It wasn't fair. How could Grace possibly be happy now that Mum and Dad were gone?

Right on cue, Astrid showed up, waving her fist in the air. "Girls! Girls! STOP THIS, NOW!" she called out from the doorway of Maggie's blue-wallpapered bedroom – the room her mother had grown up in. Maggie wondered if Astrid had yelled at Maggie's mum like this back in the Stone Age when Astrid was her nanny. "Settle down now before you give me a heart attack." Astrid patted her severe grey bun as if one strand might have fallen out of place (which it never did).

The chaos and fighting between the two sisters had been going on for six long months now. Astrid was always rolling up her sleeves and threatening some kind of punishment, which usually landed on Maggie. After Nana's children had grown up, Astrid had transitioned to baking, organizing and managing Nana's calendar. Besides helping to raise Nana's children, Astrid had seen Nana through

Grandpa's long illness and death, and had basically been Nana's right hand for the last forty years. But now Astrid was back to nannying and refereeing the sisterly outbursts, ever since that awful, rainy, moonless night last March. That's when a lorry jackknifed on the motorway and sent Maggie's parents' car down a steep embankment, killing them both.

Mum had been thrown from the car, but Maggie imagined her flying like an angel, all the way to heaven, with Dad following right behind. It was too hard to imagine much more than that. It was better to remember Mum and Dad the way Maggie had always known them: smiling, laughing in the kitchen, tucking the girls in at night and drawing fingertip hearts on their backs.

Too quickly, though, the memories were fading. Nana had moved the girls out of their smaller flat and into her much larger house. Nana's chauffeur had driven the girls to their usual school until the last school year had ended. This year the sisters transferred to a school near Nana's house. Being enrolled in a new school brought a whole new set of complicated feelings. It was the dawn of Maggie's "badditude". (Maggie had Astrid to thank for that term.) It seemed that no matter what happened, Maggie had a bad attitude about it.

To Maggie, things still felt like they were in limbo, like they were on some long holiday with Nana. Like maybe one day Mum and Dad would come back, and Maggie and Grace could move back to their *real* home. It was impossible, but Maggie desperately wanted to believe in the impossible.

After a while, Astrid was satisfied that the sisters were done fighting – for the moment – and gave them one last stern look as she headed back out of the room. But once she was out of earshot, Maggie couldn't control that familiar swell of anger.

"What's your problem?" she asked her sister.

"You!" Grace said, sticking out her tongue.

"Why do you always have to get Astrid involved?" Maggie swatted at Grace's arm.

"Ouch!" Grace wailed. "Astrid! Maggie is being mean again! Astrid, make her stop!"

The fuming Astrid quickly returned and broke up the fight once and for all with threats of no TV, mobile phones or video games for a month. "And I want to hear you apologize," Astrid commanded Maggie, even though Maggie was only *half* guilty, and even though it seemed like Maggie was *always* the one to apologize.

"I'm sorry," Maggie finally said through gritted teeth. But she wanted so much to point the finger and declare, "It wasn't just me, you know!" After all, Grace threw the first pillow.

Grace sniffed and wiped her crocodile tears. Maggie scowled at her. It was so unfair that Grace got away with everything. A disgruntled Maggie went downstairs to eat the breakfast Astrid had prepared. Nana was there too, already seated in the sunroom with her tiny cup of espresso and the newspaper.

"Good morning, Magdalene."

"Morning, Nana. Sorry about the noise–"

Nana put a finger up to Maggie's lips.

"My dear," Nana said. "A little ruckus never hurt anyone. I just want you to be a good role model. *You* are the older sister." Nana looked at Maggie pointedly.

"Ruckus indeed!" Astrid huffed. Her brows arched up into points.

Maggie glared at Astrid and leaned to kiss her grandmother's cheek. Nana's skin was smooth and soft.

Haughtily, Astrid placed a dish of steaming porridge in front of Maggie, who began to sprinkle it with brown sugar. Too much, apparently. Before she'd even shaken out a spoonful, Astrid snatched the sugar back. She was always nagging Maggie about something. So far today it was for arguing with her sister and eating too much sugar, and it wasn't even eight o'clock.

Grace arrived, skipping over to the table, and sat on Nana's lap. "Good morning!" Grace cooed. Maggie shook her head and rolled her eyes at her sister. How could she go from teeny-bopper fashion expert to little girl on grandma's lap in less than five minutes? Why could Grace still be a carefree little girl when Maggie couldn't?

It wasn't fair.

"My stars!" Nana cried, grabbing Grace around the waist. "What's this trouble I'm hearing about this morning?" she asked without a twinge of displeasure. "Pillow fights?"

"It wasn't me, I swear," Grace said innocently to Nana while looking directly at Maggie.

Maggie pushed the spoon around inside her bowl, not really eating much of the bland, sugar-free porridge. She felt tears inside, welling up like water in a tap before the knob is turned. But she had to hold them in. She'd been holding in so many tears over the past months. It felt safer to hang onto them. She was too afraid that once the crying started, it would never stop.

The old wooden cuckoo clock that had been on Nana's wall for a lifetime began to chime. Maggie slowly got up and grabbed her stuff. Three minutes (and one annoying struggle with an especially defiant curl) later, Maggie and Grace left the house through the enormous oak doors. They scooted down the stone steps to the pavement below, bags in tow.

Maggie skipped ahead a few paces, but she kept turning around to make sure that Grace was close behind. Maggie didn't want to walk with her sister, especially today, but she knew she had to.

Maggie turned at the first corner instead of the second as they usually did. They weaved in and out around other pedestrians on the street, nearly colliding with a row of silver bins. She dodged a poodle and skipped past an old woman sitting on the steps of another house. She wanted to get away – far, far away – from her sister. But the truth was that she would never just run and forget about Grace, as much as she might want to.

"Maggie, wait up!" she heard behind her.

Maggie sighed and slowed down. All at once, there was that rush of warm, sweet air again.

Bread.

Maggie followed her nose as it led her down the street to a corner bakery she hadn't noticed before. The place seemed to twinkle, though Maggie wasn't sure exactly why. The awning fluttered. Maggie quickstepped right up to the window and pressed her face to the glass.

Wow.

Inside, the walls were covered with shelves full of colourful pastries and cakes. Maggie didn't know where to look first. She'd never seen anywhere quite like this. There were dozens – no, hundreds – of cookies, cakes and breads in glass cases all over. A sign decorating the wall read: *EAT MORE CAKE*. There was so much to see. Maggie needed to get inside.

At that exact moment, as Maggie was looking in, a frizzy-red-haired woman with a kind face looked out through the glass. They locked eyes. The woman smiled and winked. Maggie smiled back, surprised. She couldn't remember the last time she'd smiled.

"MAGGIE!" a small voice barked behind Maggie. "Forget someone?"

Maggie jumped. Grace had finally caught up.

"You're supposed to wait for me," Grace whined.

"You're too slow. Besides, I could see you the whole time," Maggie fibbed.

She turned quickly to look back inside the bakery, but the smiling woman was gone. There were only tables and chairs and a chandelier that looked as if it were made of lollipops.

Grace looked inside too and soon was practically drooling on the window glass. Maggie sighed and dragged Grace away by the arm towards school.

It would only be a matter of time before the boring, friendless day officially began. But right now all Maggie could think about was the bakery and the smiling woman. For some reason, she knew she wanted – she *needed* – to come back to this place and that smiling face.

She just didn't know why.

Chapter 2

Stirring things up

Mr Keystone wasn't happy. Maggie had been to the head teacher's office twice last week. Now, on Monday, she was already back again. She had got into an argument with her science lab partner and snapped his safety goggles against his face, spilled a test tube filled with some kind of mystery liquid and then caused a fire. "Only a small fire!" she assured Mr Keystone.

Thankfully, the fire was extinguished, but the teacher's anger was not.

There was a long list of things Maggie had done wrong since she'd started at her new school. She was making quite the wrong impression.

"You see my dilemma here," Mr Keystone sighed. "We want to understand your particular ... situation, Magdalene."

Maggie lowered her head. Here was another "your-particular-situation" lecture. That was code for "Your mum and dad died and we have absolutely no idea what to say to you."

"I shouldn't have lost my temper. I know," Maggie said and then mumbled, "It's not that big a deal."

Mr Keystone rubbed his chin. "I'm afraid it is a big deal. You've been sent to my office at least five times since you started here, Magdalene. And this latest infraction involves pyrotechnics."

"The fire was an accident, I swear. It could have happened to anybody." Maggie considered blaming the science teacher for giving Year 7 pupils flammable liquids, but decided that might just get her in deeper.

"How are your counselling sessions going?" Mr Keystone asked, clearly fishing for some big important answer.

But Maggie just shrugged. She had been going to see Dr Lister, the school psychologist, twice a week, but she wasn't sure what they were really accomplishing.

At her old school, Maggie never saw the inside of the head teacher's office. She'd never had reason to. She'd always imagined it as more of a prison than an office, really. But Mr Keystone's office had fuzzy pillows on the chairs, plants along the windowsill and the walls were covered with dumb cat posters that said things like "Turn that frown upside down!"

Maggie imagined Mr Keystone's phone call to Nana's house. She saw Astrid's sour expression as she answered the call and her snippy voice would declare, "Gracie would never act this way! Gracie doesn't light fires in science lessons!" Of course not. Gracie was too busy being Adorable. (With a capital *A*, of course.)

That was the one thing that hadn't changed since the accident: Grace was the good one who got nothing but gold stars, teacher's pet status and a crew of BFFs at the lunch table. That was always the way it had been for Grace.

But Maggie had somehow become the misfit.

"Ahh," Mr Keystone stood up. "Your grandmother is finally here. Why don't you wait in the outer office, Magdalene, while she and I speak privately?"

As they passed in the doorway, Nana put her hand on Maggie's shoulder, but she didn't say anything. Maybe this was one too many outbursts. But Maggie didn't know how to control the anger that welled up inside her. She didn't know where to put everything she felt – or what to do with it when it came out.

When Nana came out of Mr Keystone's office fifteen minutes later, she didn't look Maggie in the eye. The limo ride back home took place in total silence. Nana just sat in one corner of the backseat with her eyes closed, rubbing her temples.

"I'm really sorry," Maggie blurted out after a

little while, when she couldn't stand the quiet anymore. She felt like she did nothing but apologize lately, even for stuff that wasn't her fault.

Nana turned to look at her. "I'm sorry too," she said. "But tomorrow is a new day."

At home Maggie was told to go straight up to her room by Astrid, who actually followed Maggie halfway up the stairs to make sure she obeyed. She waved her finger at Maggie as she climbed the stairs. "You have some serious thinking to do! You're better than this, Magdalene!"

Maggie collapsed on her bed with a scowl. Moon jumped onto the bed after her.

"Hey, kitty cat," Maggie whispered to Moon. She stroked her black ears and drew a circle with her finger around the white spot on her back. "Thanks for believing in me even when no one else does."

Moon purred and pressed her paws into Maggie's side. It was the perfect cat "you're welcome".

Maggie stared up at her ceiling, painted pale blue like the sky. She thought about her mother staring up at that same ceiling so many years ago. Then she remembered the science lesson again. Brady had said something to make Maggie angry – ironically something about why she looked mad all the time. Still, it had been a bad idea for Maggie to snap his goggles against his face. She knew that now. But everything was a bit of a blur. Was spilling that test tube really an accident? Or was it on purpose? She hadn't *known* it would start a fire on the Bunsen burner. And the teacher really should have seen that coming. It wasn't *all* Maggie's fault.

Still, why *did* Maggie keep getting into trouble? Nobody understood her, not even herself.

Maggie drifted off to let's-pretend-this-day-never-happened dreamland and awoke with Grace leaning over her.

"You got kicked out of school *again?* No way!" Grace said, bouncing on Maggie's bed. "What did you do this time?"

"Stop it!" Maggie pushed Grace off the bed. "I

didn't get kicked out. Mum took me out."

"Mum?" Grace sat back, stunned. "You mean ... Nana?"

"Yes," Maggie quickly corrected herself. "Of course. Duh. I was half asleep!"

Grace fell backwards. "Why did you say that? Why did you say *Mum*?"

Maggie didn't answer. They just sat there in a moment of awkward, pained silence. She wanted to reply, *Why wouldn't I say that? I miss Mum and Dad all the time, and it just slipped out. Don't YOU miss them?*

But Maggie said nothing.

Grace slowly slid off the bed. "Nana told me to tell you she has dinner ready. Well, Astrid has dinner ready. I don't think Nana actually cooks anything. Astrid made chipped beef on toast."

"Ugh, what is *that*?"

"It's pink. But it's a weird pink. Like cat sick," Grace giggled.

"*Ewww*! That is gross." Maggie couldn't help but

smile a little at Grace's funny gagging face.

"Remember Mum's dinners? She always made that yummy chicken with lemons?" Grace asked. "And her homemade fortune cookies?"

"I spent a whole Saturday baking with her once, and I couldn't make one fortune cookie fold correctly. She was the pro," Maggie said, remembering.

The two sisters, without realizing it, ended up walking downstairs to the dining room with their arms slung over each other's shoulders. A line from a song that Mum used to sing suddenly popped into Maggie's head.

I see the moon and the moon sees me

And the moon sees the one that I long to see.

Nana seemed to have forgotten all about the incident in school, because after they picked sparingly at the plates of chipped beef, she suggested they take a walk. She had read a terrific local review in the newspaper and thought they should pay a visit to the hot new bakery everyone was talking about, a place called Daisy's Desserts.

Maggie's pulse quickened. Daisy's Desserts? That was the place she'd seen earlier, the one with the lollipop chandelier that smelled like warm bread and cinnamon.

Astrid took away the dishes, and Maggie could hardly contain her excitement. She was even grinning a little, which must have looked pretty odd considering Maggie had been frowning for the better part of a year. As the threesome headed into the dusk-light to Daisy's Desserts, Astrid stayed behind. Maggie liked that part the very best of all.

Outside Daisy's Desserts, Maggie spotted a man with a guitar setting up on a small set of risers. What was going on here tonight? The band had hung a banner on the side of the shop: *BAKED LOVE*. Was that the band's name? It sounded so funny.

"Ladies and Gents," the lead singer purred into the microphone. "Feeling sweet?" The smallish crowd near the risers clapped and whistled.

People had queued up for a night of free samples. Apparently this was a regular thing on Mondays, an introduction to special items that would be baked during the week.

"It all smells heavenly!" Nana sighed. Maggie inhaled deeply. Then Nana whispered, "I wonder if their baked goods are better than Astrid's?" And she winked.

Maggie chuckled to herself. It was nice to be somewhere with Nana alone. Well, Grace was there too, but just the three of them. Family.

An oversized menu had been posted on an easel. Maggie read it, and her stomach growled a little bit louder with each item that she read. It all sounded so good.

Cinnamon buns with drizzle. Challah poppy knots. Baked sourdough loaves ...

A bright, talkative man in a white apron bounced around the crowd with a small silver tray of some tufts of bread. They smelled oven-fresh. Sweet and savoury aromas wafted around all of them like some kind of baked cloud.

"Try one!" the smiling man said.

"Hello, sir! And what is good tonight, Mr Carlos?" Nana said, reading his nametag.

"Ah, miss, *everything* is good at Daisy's Desserts. This is from a loaf of sea salt caramel raisin bread I baked just half an hour ago," Carlos said proudly.

Maggie, Grace and Nana all took a nibble of the new bread. It was soft and sweet and just a touch salty. *Wow*.

The three of them sat down at one of the tables that had been set up on the pavement outside the shop. Heat lamps kept everyone warm in the autumn chill. On each table was a white paper tablecloth and a small bucket filled with crayons. A sign had been posted nearby that caught Maggie's eye: *Draw your own sweet treat!*

Maggie and Grace decided to have a contest to see who could invent the best cupcake. After only a few moments, Grace was clearly winning – as usual. She used more colours and shapes and hers took up half the tablecloth. It had, according to Grace, thirty-two fabulous layers.

Nana went off to find a server who might get her a cup of Earl Grey tea.

When Maggie looked back down at her artwork, she saw a red crayon smudge on the paper right by her thumb. It was in the shape of a perfect heart.

"Did you–?" She started to ask Grace if she had drawn it, but someone interrupted.

"Wait! I know you!"

Maggie looked up in surprise. It was a girl from school. She was in her science lesson, but she'd never talked to Maggie before today. Maggie thought her name was Sofia something.

"OMG, you're Magdalene McAllister, who lit the fire in science, right?"

"Huh?" Grace said, looking up from her colouring. "What fire?"

"Uhhh ..." Maggie did not want Grace to know the details of what had happened today. "It was only a small fire," Maggie said with a clenched jaw.

"Ha!" Sofia laughed. "That was like the craziest and best thing that's happened since school started.

You're already like a legend in our class, and you're new here, right?"

Maggie looked sceptical. "A legend?"

"Yeah! Everyone is talking about you," Sofia gestured wildly with her hands. "*Everyone.*"

"Well, that's weird," Maggie said.

"Nah, I thought it was cool," Sofia said. "Anyway ..."

"Yeah, well ..." Maggie said, just wanting the conversation to be over. She didn't like being the centre of this kind of attention.

"My family is right over there. We're here to try out the new bakery," Sofia said. She pointed at the window. Inside a woman and younger boy sat at a table. They were digging into an enormous slice of cake.

"You don't have to stand here and talk to me," Maggie said abruptly. "Hi and bye, right?"

Without meaning to, Maggie was coming across as the meanest meanie ever. Sofia looked confused. "Okay," she mumbled. "See you at school, I guess." She walked back to her table.

"Okay..." Grace mumbled, giving Maggie an awkward look.

Just then Nana sat down with her steaming hot cup of tea. "Who was that?" she asked, looking after Sofia. "She looks nice."

"Just someone from school," Maggie mumbled.

"Oh, a friend?" Nana pressed, hopefully.

"Come on, Nana, you know I don't have any friends."

"Maggie!" Nana said. "Enough of that talk."

Maggie frowned and jabbed at a raisin that had fallen out of her bread.

"You need to start making friends," Nana said.

A woman in a speckled blue apron appeared at the table. Her nametag read DINA. She wore her dark grey hair in a long plait down her back. "Can I get anything for you ladies?" she asked.

"You certainly are busy today!" Nana said.

Dina wiped her hand across her brow. "Since the doors opened we've been swamped! People come back for seconds and bring all their friends."

"See, Magdalene," Nana said triumphantly. "You could make friends here!"

"Nana, *please*," Maggie groaned. "You're embarrassing me!"

Nana and Dina shared a laugh. "I can never seem to say the right thing to these girls," Nana said.

"Grandchildren?"

Nana nodded. They began chatting away like they'd been friends for a century.

"I've got just the thing for this pair!" Dina said, after telling Nana about all six of her grandchildren. "A bite from one of Daisy's apple bars!"

"Be a dear then and bring us one of those with three forks, please," Nana said.

"Coming right up!"

Dina zipped away, hair swinging. Grace was still absorbed in her colouring, adding layer number thirty-three to her cupcake. Maggie leaned a little closer to Nana.

"I know I always seem to be making you mad, Nana," Maggie said in a near whisper. "Is there possibly a time coming up when you will not be mad anymore?"

"Oh, Magdalene," Nana said. "I'm not mad, not really."

Nana leaned forward, pushed aside some of Maggie's flyaway curls and kissed her freckled forehead. "My darling, you just need to be more open to friendships. Next time, try being *nice* to someone who starts a conversation with you. Nanas know things, you know."

"I know," Maggie said, kissing Nana back on the cheek. They linked arms and sat close. Nana smelled like powder and roses. Maggie didn't want to let go.

And Nana was right, of course, about the whole making friends thing. Maggie knew that. But she couldn't seem to find her happy gear. She got stuck on words, tongue-tied and angry, and was well over her quota of "I'm sorrys" for the past year. Plus, every time something started to go a little bit right, Maggie would always blow it again and then feel sorry for herself, like right now. Such was the vicious cycle of the badditude.

Meanwhile, there was annoying Grace, colouring as if nothing bad had ever happened, and as if the *entire world* were her friend. It didn't make sense. How could two sisters be so different?

Nana pointed out the guitarist, who had started strumming softly. The comforting smells of brown sugar and baked bread and hot chocolate wafted through the bakery and out the open doors, accompanied by the soothing soundtrack.

Maggie listened closely, thinking she recognized the song. She gasped when she realized it was the song about the moon that her mother used to sing. Grace looked up too and met Maggie's eyes when she recognized it. It was like a love note from Mum. Nana touched Maggie's knee and squeezed gently.

When it was over, a woman in a flowered smock and faded jeans stood up to the mic – the same smiling woman Maggie had seen earlier through the shop window. She had a full head of red curls pulled back with a pink scarf. Maggie smiled at the red hair. Ginger-haired girls stick together, Mum had always said. Maggie had inherited her red hair from her mother, and she couldn't help feeling a bit of satisfaction in the fact that Grace ended up with brown curls, not red.

"Good evening, neighbours and friends," the woman said. As she began to speak, the lights inside Daisy's Desserts all flickered at once. The crowd "*oohed*" and "*ahhed*" as if there were some special effects show taking place. It almost seemed as if the woman at the mic was giving off sparks. There *was* an odd kind of electricity in the air.

"Hello and welcome! I'm Daisy," the woman said. "And *this* is my bakery." Daisy spread her arms to encompass the whole area with a big smile that seemed to say, *Can you believe my luck?* She continued, "My bakers and I have enough baked love to go around. We're here to take care of you!"

Baked love. That was the bakery's slogan, not the name of the band. Now it made sense.

Everyone applauded. The bakery had only been open for a short while and already the customers were showing their loyalty. One new customer stood up and did a jig while others clapped in rhythm. When the jig stopped, the soft hum of laughter and conversation filled the space.

The folksy guitarist kicked the tempo up a notch. Daisy placed the mic on its stand and hopped off the makeshift stage. Like fans seeking autographs, everyone was calling out for Daisy's attention. She waved to everyone around her, but to Maggie's surprise, Daisy locked eyes only with Maggie and made a beeline for their table.

"You! I know you!" Daisy said with delight.

Maggie had heard that once already this evening. She remembered Nana's wisdom: Be open, be nice, make friends.

"Are you talking to me?" Maggie asked shyly.

Daisy sat in the chair facing Maggie. "Yes, YOU. You were outside looking into my shop this morning."

Maggie couldn't believe Daisy would recognize her from that.

"You remember me?"

"I remember a lot of things," Daisy winked.

"My stars," Nana said, "You are something else. This place really *is* something special."

"I try!" Daisy said modestly and grinned.

"Daisy's Desserts really takes the cake!" Grace said.

Maggie groaned. "Seriously, Grace? Cake puns?"

Nana laughed. "And you, my dear Daisy, are like a pot of gold at the end of this rainbow."

"Wait ..." Daisy paused. "What did you say?"

"You are like a pot of gold at the end of this rainbow," Nana repeated. "I've never been somewhere where I felt so welcomed. Right, girls?"

"That's crazy," Daisy said. "My own Nana Belle used to say those *exact* words to me all the time. She called me a pot of gold ..."

"Well, your Nana Belle was one clever woman," Nana said and nodded her head firmly. "Like me, if I do say so myself. I was just telling my granddaughter that nanas know things."

"Yes, they do," Daisy said, nodding. Maggie thought she saw Daisy's eyes get misty for a moment.

As soon as the four had introduced themselves to each other, a baker with a beautiful silver bouffant appeared. "I'm Babs. Dina sent me," she drawled. "She's dealing with a kitchen situation at the moment. She thought you might need more than one of these," she said with a giggle and set down a plate stacked with apple bar bites.

"Bravo!" Daisy clapped her hands together. "The apple bars are here. Enjoy, on the house! Come by again when you need a little sugar, okay?" And she tapped Maggie gently on the head as she whirled away.

"We will!" Grace said cheerily. "She's nice," she whispered as Daisy disappeared.

Even though the apple bars were "on the house", Nana left enough of a tip to cover all the food times two. Someone with a new business needed support from the customers, she said, and Nana was always generous when it came to cash.

Maggie turned and looked into the bakery to see if she could catch a glimpse of Sofia. She caught Sofia's eye, but she and her family were on their way out. Sofia raised up a hand as if to wave. Maggie hesitated and then did the same, but it was too late. Sofia was gone.

Maybe Nana was right. Was the real reason why things kept getting so messed up for Maggie because she couldn't seem to remember how to act normally around people? Or because of her stupid badditude? Was that what was standing between Maggie and the rest of the world, like some kind of keep-out fence?

Maggie wanted to run after her, to see if she could catch up with Sofia. But she knew there was no point. Besides, something else seemed to be tugging at Maggie. It wasn't her sister Grace, for once. It was just a feeling, strange and new, that something inside this place had the power to rub away her sadness, just a bit. How could a bakery do that? She wanted to stay forever.

But of course, just as she was thinking that, Grace sang out, "Last one home is a rotten egg!" and smacked Maggie on the back as she got up from the table.

Nana promised they'd be back really soon. Maggie planned to come back on her own even sooner.

Chapter 3

The great hair don't

When she got ready for school on Tuesday, Maggie decided to dress up a bit more than usual. She was feeling brighter, somehow, more optimistic, since their visit to Daisy's the night before. She replaced her normal sweatshirt with a wool dress and boots. She put her hair into two thick French plait loops on the top of her head. She decided that an unusual hairstyle and funky shoes might give her a fresh start. Maybe she'd connect better with people at school. Or maybe even look and feel as cool as Daisy from the bakery.

Plus, Dad had always complimented Maggie whenever she got all dressed up. Maggie could almost hear his voice right now.

"Oooh! That fancy hair makes you look like a runway model!" Grace said at breakfast. She ran up to her bedroom to grab some tortoise shell clips Nana had bought in Paris. She loaned them to Maggie to complete the look. Then Grace snapped a pic with her phone.

But Astrid didn't approve. "Magdalene, your hair looks like a bird's nest," she said as she cleared away the breakfast dishes.

"I'm trying something new, Astrid," Maggie insisted. She poked the clips into place, then she put on a little lip gloss.

"I think you looked fine before," Astrid replied. "And *make-up*?"

"It's not make-up; it's just lip gloss," Maggie said.

"Well, I don't know how I feel about that," Astrid said with furrowed brows.

"Astrid!" Grace whined. "I don't get to wear make-up. Why does Maggie?"

"It's *not* make-up," Maggie said again. "Stop

calling it what it isn't." Then Maggie explained that she was trying the new look as a way to turn over a new leaf at school. Maybe if she looked like she cared, she could start acting like she cared too.

Astrid still wasn't sure about the lip gloss, but she gave Maggie credit where credit was due. "I admire your efforts to gain favour. Just don't get into trouble again, *please*," Astrid said. "Your Nana has been so upset. It's not healthy for her. Or me."

Maggie sighed. "I am going to do better. I swear."

"Ladies don't swear!" Astrid cried.

"I meant, I'll be good!" Maggie said, exasperated.

Nana blew into the room wearing one of her beautiful cream-coloured silken kimonos. "Did I hear you correctly?" she asked. "Did I hear you say you'll be *good*?"

"Nana," Grace interrupted. "Since Maggie has on lip gloss, can I wear some too?"

"Well," Nana said. "Let's take that up some other time." She turned to Maggie. "You're a beautiful young woman, Magdalene, and I'm glad to see you're showing that side of yourself today. Beautiful *inside* and out," she emphasized. "Your mother and father would be so proud."

Maggie sighed. Thinking about Mum and Dad was putting a lump in Maggie's throat. But she held her head up high and took a deep breath. No tears.

As she walked into school that morning, Maggie searched for Sofia. She wanted to apologize ... or something. The encounter in the bakery had been awkward, and Maggie had only herself to blame.

Sofia was nowhere to be seen, but everyone in the corridor seemed aware of Maggie. She realized too late that her plan to show she had a new and improved attitude was also like wearing a big sign that said, "Hey, everyone, look at me!" Someone said she looked like she had cinnamon buns on her head, like Princess Leia only up on top. Maggie instantly regretted not wearing the usual old curly mess of a ponytail.

Worst of all, she couldn't take her hair *out* of the knotted buns now, because it would be too crazy loose. She'd look like she'd stuck her fingers in an electrical socket.

Thankfully, Maggie made it all the way to lunch without any major embarrassments. She'd got a lot of funny looks, but she had succeeded in going all morning without getting in trouble or sticking her foot in her mouth. In the canteen, she situated herself at one end of a long green table. But sitting down by herself, the swell of being friendless hit her all over again. Was everyone in the entire school avoiding her? How was she supposed to turn over a new leaf if no one gave her a chance? People rushed from here to there with trays of food, but none came over to sit with her.

The over-baked brownie on Maggie's tray just sat there like a hockey puck. She was willing to bet big money that it tasted like fake chocolate or maybe even dirt. It definitely would never measure up to the brownies that Daisy probably made.

Even though she was lonely, Maggie was also a little relieved that no one sat with her.

It was so much work making friends. But then, out of nowhere, two girls slid their trays onto Maggie's table.

"Is it okay if we sit here?" the tall girl in the pink jumper asked. The colour was actually pretty close to Astrid's chipped beef, but somehow this girl made the colour look good.

Maggie shrugged. "I don't think so. I mean— totally. Yeah. Of course. Go ahead."

The other girl smiled. "Cool. Thanks."

"Aren't you in my maths set?" the tall girl asked. "I'm Candy."

Wait! Candy is really your name? Maggie thought to herself. Thankfully, however, what she said out loud was, "Candy is a cool name."

The other girl smiled. "I'm Britt. You're Magdalene McAllister, right? That girl from the science fire? Nice hair."

Maggie was pretty sure Britt was giving her an actual compliment and not a sarcastic one. She wanted to pinch herself. *These girls were actually talking to her? And they knew her name? And they liked her hair? Where was the hidden camera?*

"Are you wearing Think Pink?" Candy asked. "I love that lip gloss!"

Maggie tried hard not to have a big, goofy smile on her face, to play it cool, but one little smile sneaked out. "Yeah, it's so ... glossy," she said, puckering. She couldn't believe she'd said something so dumb, but the girls didn't seem to notice.

They talked a little bit about their maths set, and about Mr Keystone's corny jokes during assembly. Maggie was so happy just to be talking to other girls. Any talking would do, even conversations about maths! Plus, they mentioned her plaited buns *twice* – in a good way!

"Over here!" Britt waved someone else over. It was a lot of pressure, meeting new girls like this, but Maggie and her new attitude were doing okay so far. Nana said she could do this – and here she was. For the first time in a long time, Maggie felt like maybe she was making new friends.

The girls started jabbering to the other girl before she even sat down. Maggie turned around to see who it was.

It was Sofia – the same Sofia she'd seen at Daisy's Desserts the day before. The same Sofia she'd *been really rude to.* And the same Sofia looked just as surprised to see Maggie sitting at a table with *her* friends.

"Hey, sit here," Candy said, patting the bench next to her and across from Maggie. "This is ..."

"Yeah, I know. Maggie McAllister from science." Sofia smiled tightly. "Hi and bye. Right?" She mimicked Maggie's dumb line from the bakery. "I think I'm going to sit at *this* end." Sofia plunked her tray down at the opposite end of the table from Maggie.

Maggie suddenly felt her badditude click on again.

Candy and Britt looked confused by Sofia's move, but Sofia whispered something and they all started talking at the other end of the table. No one said another word to Maggie.

Ouch. Maggie knew she probably deserved that for how she'd treated Sofia the day before. If there was ever a time to apologize, now was the time.

But she didn't. She didn't know how.

Maggie probably could have tried to rejoin their conversation. But she couldn't think of anything to say, now that Sofia was here, reminding her of her screw-ups.

And so she was alone, again. It was no use sitting there, because no one was planning to say much of anything else to her. That much was clear. Maggie stood up with her tray. The other girls mumbled a goodbye, only glancing up from their conversation briefly. *At least they mumbled something,* Maggie thought.

She adjusted the bun plaits on top of her head and tried to act like none of it bothered her. She heard Dad's voice: "Keep your head held high."

Unfortunately, her brownie plate slipped off her tray and clattered to the floor. She dropped a fork too, and everyone started clapping, making fun of her. Then a boy at a nearby table called out, "Nice hairdo!" The boy next to him said, "You mean nice hair *don't*!" Then the whole table of boys laughed hysterically.

Maggie felt her knees buckle. The badditude was *definitely* back, and she felt like flinging her tray at the table of obnoxious boys.

But then someone called out, "Shut up, moron," and they weren't talking about Maggie. They were talking about the boy who'd made the mean comment.

Maggie turned and saw the person who spoke up.

No way. Sofia?

The funny part was that Sofia did it so casually. She didn't make a big deal out of it at all. In fact, she looked away when she said it. When the boys laughed, Sofia gave them a bad look too.

Sofia stuck up for Maggie.

It made perfect sense to go back to the lunch

table and thank Sofia, apologize for yesterday and then throw herself in front of the girls and ask them to be her BFFs. But instead, Maggie ran out of the lunchroom and headed straight for her locker. She hit a flight of stairs, almost-tears welling up. Then she burst out through swinging doors into a corridor, collided with a group of younger pupils and nearly slammed right into her own sister.

"Maggie!" Grace said in surprise, not used to seeing her sister during the day.

Maggie sniffed. There was no way she was going to cry now. NO WAY.

"Maggie, what's the matter?"

"Nothing, I'm fine," Maggie lied, wiping her nose on her sleeve. "I have to get to my locker. Get out of my way, okay?"

"But," Grace said, grabbing Maggie's sleeve. "Hold up. You look weird." Grace's friends were there too, and they all looked at Maggie with big eyes.

"I said I'm fine."

"Your face is so puffy." Grace wouldn't let up.

"Is that supposed to make me feel better?" Maggie snapped.

Grace looked a little hurt, but Maggie didn't care. "I have to go to my locker, okay? Can you please get out of my way?"

Grace nodded. "Okay, I was just ..."

"JUST get out of my way. I will see you later."

Maggie headed quickly off towards the end of the corridor. She could hear Grace call after her, "I'll meet you in the lobby after last period, okay? *Byeeee!*"

Once again, Gracie was just sailing through her day, while Maggie was a walking disaster. *It wasn't fair.*

Just then, the school intercom buzzed. Maggie couldn't really hear what Mr Keystone was saying. Something about an assembly, or was it about being friendly? His announcements were always so garbled. Then the bell to change lessons rang, and pupils flooded into the corridor. By now Maggie was at her locker. She grabbed her books and raced downstairs to Social Studies, avoiding making eye contact with anyone.

The urge to sob had passed, but that didn't mean Maggie felt better. Sitting at the back of the room, she had a lot of trouble concentrating. She found herself staring out of the window again, just like she'd done at home, and doodling mindlessly in the margins of her notebook.

First she drew random squiggles. Then she wrote her name over and over. Then she drew cats like her own Moon, cats with dots and splotches and stripes. Cats with dark fur. Cats with stars for eyes. Cats with far too many whiskers. She could not focus on the dates and dead kings and queens her teacher was droning on about. Instead, she was over-thinking, feeling everything at once: angry, sad, then spaced out, angry, sad, then spaced out. Over and over, again and again. But this was nothing new. This was how things had been for months.

Ever since the accident.

Maybe this was just how she would feel forever.

She felt stupid for thinking that a new outfit and hairdo could change anything about her life.

At the end of the lesson, Maggie stopped back at her locker to swap her books. She had one free period, and then the day would be over. It couldn't be over soon enough for Maggie.

"Hey," a voice said.

Maggie turned. Sofia was standing there.

"I'm sorry about lunch," Sofia blurted.

"Huh? Why are *you* sorry?" Maggie asked.

"I felt so bad about it afterwards. About the way I acted. I should have just sat across from you at the lunch table and not made a big deal."

"Wait. No," Maggie said. "You stuck up for me."

"Yeah, those boys are real idiots," Sofia said. "Someone needs to shut them up. I seized the opportunity."

They both smiled.

"Well ..." Maggie didn't know what to say.

Sofia helped again. "You're welcome."

"Thanks," Maggie said softly at last.

"Anyone who lights the science room on fire should be defended at all costs. We need you to keep school interesting," Sofia teased.

Maggie smiled. "I'm not trying to be interesting, trust me. I just, well, I don't always ..."

Sofia seemed to understand. "Sit with us at lunch tomorrow?" she asked. "I promise I won't move to the other end of the table."

Maggie shrugged and smiled. "Okay."

"See you tomorrow then," Sofia said, raising her hand up for a high five. Maggie slapped it back. What else could she do?

For the first time in a very long time, Maggie felt a little glimmer of something like happy.

Chapter 4

Give me butterflies

Grace was waiting by the lobby trophy case after the final bell rang, as instructed. Maggie was running late.

When she got there, Grace said with a look of surprise, "You look happy again. And what took you so long?"

"Nothing. Why are you so nosy?"

"Where are we going, and why is it a secret?" Grace asked. As part of Maggie's new and improved attitude, she had promised that morning that she'd take Grace somewhere special after school for a treat. Grace could hardly stop moving, bouncing from one pink trainer to the other.

"Not a secret. Just somewhere sweet," Maggie said. "Remember?"

"Daisy's Desserts?" Grace guessed. Maggie nodded and Grace pumped her fist in the air. "*Yesssss!*"

They rushed out together, through the school's front doors and past the queue of traffic in front of school. Maggie and Grace pulled on their backpacks and headed down the street on foot. There was plenty to explore on the way to the bakery. Maggie called it an adventure.

Recently Grace had noticed a new stylish clothes shop that just opened up. It was called Bella's Bazaar, and they had children's clothes too.

As they passed it today, Grace squealed, "Mags, look! Now it's the *Butterfly* Bazaar!" She bopped up and down with excitement and pointed. The entire shop had been decorated with butterflies in different shapes and sizes and colours. Words ran from one side of the window to the other: *YOU GIVE ME BUTTERFLIES.*

Grace begged to go inside and try on some of the funky outfits they had on display: T-shirts with big words written in glitter letters, stretchy jeggings, cute dresses and cozy hoodies with fake fur trim. But Maggie wasn't in the mood for shopping.

"You have enough clothes," she said to Grace. "Come on."

"No, please!" Grace insisted. "Just for a few minutes. You promised."

"When did I promise?" Maggie asked, shaking her head.

"You said it was an adventure, remember? Pretty please with vanilla whipped cream and a cherry?"

"Fine. Three minutes. Seriously. I'm timing this."

They went inside together. Maggie pulled out her phone and set the timer for five minutes. (She decided to be generous.) Instantly, Grace found an enormous basket of scarves and quickly pulled out one with purple dragonflies on it.

All the scarves were decorated with crazy, colourful patterns. These clothes really *were* fun.

But Maggie had her eye on her phone.

Three minutes and counting until destination Daisy's!

"Gracie!" Maggie warned. "Time's almost up."

The saleswoman was lurking nearby. "Can I help you find something?" she smiled sweetly, but Maggie knew it was fake. She also knew it was only a matter of time before Grace started getting silly.

Right on cue, her sister disappeared behind a rack of dresses.

"Gracie," Maggie said. "Time to go."

"Do you think you can please keep away from the racks?" the saleswoman said nervously.

Grace reappeared in an instant with her arms stuffed. Clothes and hangers were strewn all over the floor.

"Grace! What are you doing?" Maggie cried.

"You'll have to hand all that over now, please," the saleswoman insisted, fake smile gone. At that exact moment Grace tripped on a dangling hanger and fell backwards into a billowing rack of harem trousers.

"Whoops," Grace said. "Luckily, I think the clothes broke my fall."

"Grace!" Maggie scolded.

"Where is your mother?" the saleswoman demanded.

Maggie and Grace just stared back at her in stunned silence. *Why did everyone always assume they had a mother?*

Maggie saw Gracie's face fall. Her sister had been having fun playing dress-up, and now this stuffy woman in fancy clothes burst her bubble by reminding Grace of the worst thing in their lives.

"We were just looking around," Maggie countered, trying to change the subject, gently squeezing Grace's shoulders so she wouldn't say anything.

"I think you need to leave," the woman said, glaring at them. "Now."

Maggie felt her stomach ache, and it wasn't butterflies or anything good.

They needed to get out of there before they got into even bigger trouble. The badditude threatened to surface like bubbling lava, but Maggie bit her tongue.

Grace was the one who blew her top as they left the store. "I'm telling Nana! I want that scarf!" she declared, stomping down the street.

"We are *not* giving that woman any of our business," Maggie said, but Grace was already distracted by another colourful shop, and suddenly the incident seemed forgotten.

Forgotten so soon? How could Grace just move on? And why couldn't Maggie?

A few doors down from Bella's Bazaar was an old corner shop with a large, peeling sign in the window: *B.K. ROOTS TONICS, HERBALS & REMEDIES*. The words were painted in the centre between a mortar and pestle and a vial of some perfume. Maggie explained to Grace that this was an apothecary shop – an old-fashioned chemists. This one had new objects mixed in with the old.

"Cool! Let's go in!" Grace cried, reaching for the old brass door handle.

"I don't know ..." Maggie said cautiously. It did look cool, like something from another era. There were all sorts of tin signs and a worktop with spinning stools. They could see that much from the door. A large plaque at the front read "*Est. 1885*" alongside a smaller sign that said, "*Sundries*".

"What's a sundry?" Grace asked. "I want one!"

Maggie rolled her eyes. "Of course you do."

They poked their noses through the door and then stepped across the threshold. Immediately Grace bumped into a lamp, causing it to flicker, and then, turning, she thwacked her backpack against a stand of coloured bottles. The entire thing came crashing down onto the floor. Thankfully, everything was plastic or it would have been an epic disaster.

A woman with a flame of fake orange hair and a perma-sneer rushed straight over, waving her arms like a maniac. "Look what you've done! Look at this mess! Where are your parents?"

There it was again: *Parents.*

"I'm so sorry," Maggie said, kneeling to help pick up the bottles. "It was just an accident. My sister didn't know–"

"There are no accidents," the woman said angrily. "Out of my shop!"

Maggie felt her whole face go pink. An older customer in the back of the shop peered at them over her black-framed glasses.

"Let's go, Gracie," Maggie said. "Now."

As they slinked out of the shop, Grace started giggling. "She was REALLY mad!"

And once again, Grace was laughing while Maggie was left feeling like she had her own personal storm cloud overhead. Grace had turned a short simple walk from school into an adventure all right – a trouble-dodging adventure. They continued on down the street.

Even though they'd lived in this neighbourhood for many months now, Grace's enthusiasm for all the new shops hadn't diminished. She pointed at a neon coat hanger sign positioned outside the dry-cleaners. After that she spotted a pizzeria called The Dough Boys with a queue of hungry children crammed inside for a slice after school. A crazy painted first floor door had a box near it with a dozen call buttons. There were different offices rented here, including D'Amicci's Art Gallery on the second floor and Mona the Mindreading Mystic on the third.

Of course, Grace wanted to go inside.

"We are not going to the art gallery! Or getting our fortunes told!" Maggie said, pulling Grace away. She didn't want her sister causing any other pricey disasters.

"Why not?" Grace moaned. "Maybe she can read our palms!"

"I don't need a mystic mind reader to tell me that my life stinks and will always stink," Maggie grumbled, her good mood having faded entirely.

Not far from the bakery, just down a side street,

was a big sign for Weller's Book Shoppe. Grace turned the corner and walked towards it. This, like the apothecary, had been here for about a thousand years. There were corners (and cobwebs) in Weller's that had yet to be discovered, it seemed. Grace peered through the large front window.

"What a place!" Grace cried. "Maggie, look!"

"What a mess!" Maggie said. All she saw were aisles and piles of books, each more topsy-turvy than the next. This was a shop someone could get lost in – *literally*. And it definitely was a shop where Grace would knock things over and cause trouble, and possibly get killed by a collapsing bookshelf.

"We *have* to go into this bookshop. It's so mega!" cried Grace.

"Come on," Maggie said. "Maybe later."

"Can I help you?" a smiling, older gentleman appeared at the door. Unlike all the other shopkeepers, this one seemed *eager* to let Maggie and Grace inside. He didn't issue any warnings to "keep your hands to yourself or else". He introduced himself as Mr Weller the Third and stroked his bushy grey beard thoughtfully. "I am sure we've got something for you young ladies to read," he said.

Maggie said, "Um, this is super nice, but we were just–"

"COMING IN! Totally!" Grace interrupted and bounded past the old man.

When they were small, Mum used to always take the girls to the children's reading room at the library. Sometimes she'd even dress them up in costumes like on Superhero Day or Fairy Tale Day. Grace would always get distracted during story time, pulling every book off the shelf but never reading any of them.

Just like then, Grace's attention was divided now too. While she was staring open-mouthed up at ceiling-height bookshelves, she nearly walked straight into a table covered with dusty display books. Luckily the table only shook a little and there was no repeat performance of the earlier fiasco.

Old framed maps were tacked right onto the

bookshelves and every exposed wall. There was a section devoted entirely to atlases. There were signs handwritten in thick black marker indicating the various sections of the shop, with labels like *"Biography"* and *"Nature"*.

"What's that?" Grace asked curiously, pointing up at a large red book high on a shelf. Maggie could tell her sister was planning to settle in and get comfy in the chairs that were positioned haphazardly around the shop, but Maggie stopped her.

"We need to go," Maggie whispered to Grace. "Remember our mission?"

"I want to stay! I see a book on 1960s fashion!" Grace cried. "Ooh! And they have a whole section on kitties!"

Maggie groaned. A walk from school that should have taken ten minutes to the bakery had turned into an hour-long detour. They still had homework. Astrid would be expecting them soon. And Maggie just wanted to go to Daisy's.

She took Grace by the arm. "We *need* to go. Do

you really want Astrid to freak out on us again?"

"She mostly freaks out on you, not me," Grace said. Maggie couldn't argue with that one. "I suppose we can go," Grace finally said with a sigh.

The sisters thanked Mr Weller, who gave them an odd salute, and they headed out the door again.

When they finally arrived at Daisy's, it didn't look half as busy as it had been the night before. Daisy had installed oversized potted plants near the outdoor seating area, but most people were sitting inside today since it was getting chillier.

Breathless, Maggie and Grace stumbled into the bakery and collapsed into two blue upholstered chairs around a little end table. Maggie couldn't help but smile at the happy surroundings, and she let out a long sigh of contentment.

Babs came over right away. "Well, if it isn't the curly girls, Grace and ... Maggie, right?"

The "curly girls" nodded. Maggie wasn't surprised that Babs had remembered Grace's name first.

"Take a look and tell me what you want to order," she said. "Key Lime Tartelettes are today's special."

Grace made a funny face. "That sounds sour!" she exclaimed and jumped up to the counter to find something she liked better. Babs helped her to decide on a ginger whipper snapper.

"*You* are the original whipper snapper, aren't you?" Maggie heard Babs say to Grace. Grace giggled, and Maggie thought that yes, Grace certainly had the zing of a ginger snap. As usual, Grace was commanding centre stage.

It was the same wherever they went, and it didn't seem fair.

At least here, in the bakery, Maggie felt more hopeful about things, and not just because everything in sight was sugar-coated. It was tough to dislike a place with sparkly lights on the ceiling and the soft hum of orchestral music in the background and enough chocolate to ice the whole city. She glanced around, hoping maybe she might spot Sofia here again.

Grace bopped back to the table with the ginger snaps. She had one for Maggie too.

"Thanks," Maggie said as she bit into her cookie. And something about that sweet bite of cookie and being at Daisy's brightened Maggie's mood again. "Today isn't so bad, is it? Crazy, but fun, right?" she said to Grace.

Grace raised an eyebrow. "Did you forget that that woman booted us out of her shop? And the apoth-a-derry? Eek!" She pulled her lips back in a guilty but comical grimace.

"Yeah, you're annoying, all right," Maggie said, nudging her sister. "But fun too."

Grace smiled. "Of course I am. I'm the funnest!"

"Funnest?" Maggie laughed. "Don't push it. And that isn't even a word."

"Ha!" Grace grinned. "That's what Mum always–" Grace stopped herself.

Maggie nodded and their chatter stopped. *Mum.*

Mum had always corrected their mistakes. She

was a stickler. It drove the girls mad when Mum would wag her finger at them and say, "If you keep talking like that, no one will ever take you seriously."

Maggie imagined Mum's full face with sparkling green eyes. Mum never made Maggie and Grace feel bad about anything   well, except their grammar. But even those were gentle reminders, never scolding.

"I miss her," Grace said. It was the first time Maggie had heard her say anything like that in many months. Maybe those comments from the shop owners had bugged Grace more than she'd let on.

"I bet she misses us too," Maggie added.

"How is that possible?" Grace asked.

Maggie reached out and touched one of Grace's curls lightly. "I don't mean she *actually* misses us, like in present tense. It's just an expression. She's somewhere in heaven looking down. Or whatever."

"Yeah," Gracie nodded. "She definitely is."

And just then two little somethings fluttered down onto their small table, like paper snow from the ceiling. *Was this another love note?* Maggie wondered, remembering that mysterious crayon heart on her paper from the night before. She got a very strange but wonderful feeling. Almost magical.

"Fancy seeing you here," Daisy said, offering a tray with small cups of strawberry limeade. "Try it!"

Grace grabbed a cup straight away.

"We've got a lime theme in case you missed it. Not sure how popular it'll be," Daisy went on. "It might need more sugar!" she laughed, eyeing Grace's puckering lips as she sipped the drink.

Daisy's curly hair was poking out from under a thick headband. She had full red lips like a film star. Today, she didn't look like a baker at all. Then again, what was a baker supposed to look like? Silver-haired Babs looked a little out of place too, like she belonged in some 1950s diner and not a hip bakery. And Dina with her long plait had a look all her own too. But somehow everyone belonged. There was a place for everyone.

Including Maggie.

"Can I have a sample too?" Maggie asked Daisy.

"Of course," Daisy said, placing a second mini-cup onto the table before turning around and slinking away in a pair of too-cool red cowboy boots. Daisy had a lot of fun secrets, Maggie guessed.

"Thanks," Maggie called out. She took a sour-sweet slurp from the cup and sucked in her cheeks. "Whew!" she exclaimed. "Okay, ready to get to work, Grace? I have a load of maths and science tonight. You?"

"Not much. Just spelling."

"Lucky," Maggie said with a playful nudge and then pulled her enormous black binder from her backpack. Something felt different today for the first time in a long time. Maybe it was Sofia. Or maybe it was realizing that Grace hadn't forgotten Mum and Dad after all. Or maybe it was this place? A little sugar, as Daisy had said? Maybe Mum and Dad really were watching over them right now.

Chapter 5

Making magic

Maggie and Grace started going to the bakery more often, and it changed things between them, at least for a while. It seemed as if a fog had lifted, even at home. And less fighting between the girls meant Astrid and Nana were in tip-top spirits. Astrid went two whole days without having anything to yell at them about.

Things at school mellowed a little bit too. Sofia kept her promise to include Maggie at lunch with Britt and Candy. Most of the time Maggie just ate her sandwich while they did most of the talking, but it still felt good to be included.

Maggie's grades were looking up too. She

felt proud earning more Bs and even a few As. Mr Keystone was delighted that Maggie had not been to his office in weeks. It was as if the badditude had gone into hibernation. At last.

One Sunday Maggie and Grace were sitting in the greenhouse room at Nana's house. It was a huge room up on the second floor that had once been an old-fashioned conservatory. Nana had renovated it with pots and planters and even piped-in music. She'd read somewhere that plants grew better with Beethoven's Fifth Symphony playing.

Astrid kept her eye on greenhouse things along with Nana's gardener. There were lettuces, tomatoes, squash, courgettes and other vegetables that grew all year round. And Astrid was teaching Maggie and Grace to tend the herb garden, which included basil, oregano and chives.

The herb garden had first been planted years before by Mum, when she was just a girl. Maggie thought there was something amazing about sticking her hands into the same dirt Mum had touched years earlier. Sometimes the plants even came back, plants that Mum had planted so long ago. They were like tiny living love notes from her.

Photographs were love notes too. Downstairs in the large study, Nana had shelves of albums and the girls would sometimes sit down in Nana's enormous red leather chairs and flip through the photographs for hours. Nana had stories to go with every picture.

Those albums contained shots of everyone who had visited them at the house or at Nana's country house, with its ice skating pond and tyre swings.

Maggie turned to one page with a large photograph of a young girl on a pony.

"Who's that, Nana?" she asked.

Nana smiled broadly. "Your mother, of course. On Nugget. How she loved that horse."

Maggie flipped to more photos of Mum as a young girl taken in all sorts of locations, with her brother and sister, doing all sorts of things: sailing a boat, painting a canvas and standing in the middle of a field of purple flowers, hands on her hips, red hair blowing in the wind.

"She looks like you, sis," Grace said, leaning in close to get a better look.

"Yeah," Maggie said, feeling a twinge of sadness inside.

There were many black and white photographs of Grandpa Joe too. The girls never knew him because he had died years before the girls were born.

Of course there was Mum with Dad when he came on the scene. Nana had pages of photos from when Dad first took Mum out on a date, from their honeymoon, from every moment of their relationship.

Maggie liked one picture best: It showed Mum holding newborn Maggie in her arms, looking lovingly at her while Dad wrapped his arm around Mum's shoulder and leaned in. Mum and Dad both looked exhausted but perfect – dark under-eye circles, messy hair and all.

After the accident, Maggie and Grace had examined these same photographs longingly, wishing for what they couldn't have, thinking Mum and Dad would somehow turn up and take them back home. They imagined themselves back in their old, smaller flat with the sticky windowpanes and the large-planked wooden floors and the messy, humming kitchen. Because after all, pictures take a person from here to back there. Pictures bring everything back, fresh, crisp and loved.

But seeing these photos was hard, and Maggie only looked at them behind closed doors. It was her unspoken rule. Mum and Dad were tucked away in snapshots and the wedding photograph on Nana's wall. That was where they had to stay. No one else could have them. Maggie didn't ever speak about her parents at school, not even to Sofia. Some secrets were better kept under lock and key.

Maggie and Grace's visits to the bakery slowed when the days got shorter. An early snow arrived in the city, and there were all sorts of excuses that kept them away. With the colder temps, the sisters' truce seemed to cool as well, and the bickering started up again.

One afternoon, Nana's driver brought Astrid to pick them up instead of letting the girls walk home. Grace was meant to be trying out a new ballet class.

"Get in the limo," Astrid ordered Maggie. She was never fond of small talk, not even when Maggie had a *good* attitude.

"Astrid, do I have to go to Grace's class?" Maggie asked. "I'll walk home instead. I have loads of homework I need to finish." She had other plans today that did not include watching her sister pretend she was the star of *Swan Lake*.

"Get in the car, Mags," Grace boomed. "I can't be late for my first class!"

Astrid held the door open, but Maggie still wasn't giving in. She'd made up her mind.

"I can wait for you two to get back," Maggie suggested, trying a positive approach instead of a negative one. A little sugar, like Daisy said. "I'll go over to the bakery and get some reading done. I have an essay to write and some maths and–"

"Fine," Astrid huffed. "But be home by five! And don't get into any trouble."

Why did Astrid have to rub that in? Maggie hadn't been in trouble in weeks now. Then again, for Maggie there always seemed to be the looming chance that everything would blow up into another hot-lava mess. That's how it usually worked, and Astrid seemed all too eager to remind her of that.

Maggie tried not to feel bad. Instead she held up her two fingers like she was making a promise and smiled broadly at Astrid who was rolling up the limo window.

"No fires," Maggie said. "I promise."

Maggie watched the limo pull away and then headed over to the bakery all by herself, bag of homework slung over her shoulder. This little taste of freedom was almost as delicious as Daisy's apple bars. The walk there from school was quick – and so different without Grace sticking her face on every shop window to see inside. Maggie didn't have to pay the same kind of attention, and she could let her mind wander and people watch, not just Grace watch.

As soon as she stepped across the threshold at Daisy's, Maggie felt her heart give a little leap. A feeling of calm enveloped her immediately. Best of all, a familiar smile spread across her face like an old friend.

There was a decent chance Maggie might run into someone from school at Daisy's Desserts. And what better way to get a set of word problems done than by inhaling a carrot cake muffin smothered in coconut cream while you worked? The bakery offered new surprises each visit. Maggie had a few pounds stuffed into her backpack for baked emergencies just like this one.

A perfect corner table near an overflowing bookshelf was available at the far end of the cookie counter. The table was distressed and painted all different colours along with its chairs.

Maggie sat down and got to work – or at least took out her work and stared at it for a little while. She searched the place for Babs or Dina, who usually swept in to chat with Maggie whenever she came. But today she didn't see either of them around. In fact, the place was quieter than usual. Quiet should have been ideal working conditions for homework, but the aroma of chocolate was a little distracting.

Then the best distraction of all came by: Daisy.

"What are you working on?" Daisy asked, leaning down for a peek.

Maggie shrugged. "Maths. But I can't focus."

"Where's your sister today?" she asked.

"Dance class," Maggie answered, hoping that Daisy wasn't disappointed that centre-of-attention Grace wasn't there to provide entertainment.

"Well good, because, you know, I've been waiting for a chance to talk to you," Daisy said thoughtfully. "Since you're on your own and the place is a little quiet today, do you think maybe you could help me?"

"*Me?* Help you?" Maggie gulped. "What do you need?"

"I'll show you. Follow me," Daisy said with a smile.

Maggie had a moment of panic. She wasn't capable of helping Daisy, was she? What if she messed something up? What if she really did set another fire?

Daisy helped Maggie stuff all her notebooks back into her school bag. Then she squeezed Maggie's shoulder and led her towards the kitchen. With that gentle contact, everything inside the bakery – and inside Maggie – brightened. The cupcake icing colours turned radioactive; the teeny stained glass windows up along one baking rack shimmered like a kaleidoscope; and the checked linoleum patches of floor vibrated with bright blue. It was as if Maggie could feel the colours and the smells. There was mint and banana and, of course, chocolate. There was cinnamon and lemon and spice. And, towards the kitchen, an amazing warm buttered bread scent swirled around Maggie like a hug sent from heaven.

"You haven't been back here before, have you?" Daisy asked, opening the wide set of double doors that led to the kitchen.

Maggie shook her head slowly and then paused before walking through.

"Whoa," she breathed. It was magnificent. The back of the bakery was so totally ... shiny! Everywhere was stainless steel, silver and reflecting, like a dozen mirrors at every angle. And it was even *bigger* than the front of the bakery. Bakers were busy at every counter, rolling, kneading, icing and slicing.

"This is like a fun house!" Maggie laughed.

"A little bit, you're right," Daisy said, laughing too. "So are you ready for some fun?"

"I think so," Maggie said cautiously, even though inside she was screaming, *Yes! Yes!* She didn't know quite what to think. It was as if she'd fallen into another dimension. That's what it felt like. She was Alice down the rabbit hole, *EAT ME* and *DRINK ME* signs up ahead. Maggie couldn't wait to discover more enchantment within this wonderful place.

There was a preparation area filled with dozens of bins for flour and sugar and who knew what else. A large case held fondant sheets in every colour. One entire wall was covered with rows of colour-coded sprinkles and other toppings.

Up on the wall in the back were photos, artfully framed close-ups of chocolate truffle squares dusted with sugar and doughnuts just out of the fryer. Then Maggie saw black and white portraits of the bakers too. There was a picture of Babs with her big up-do, dressed like a real-life film star from a long time ago. Carlos was there with his four children climbing all over him. Dina was posing on a beach somewhere with her long hair loose in the wind, her bare feet in the sand. And there was Daisy in her photo, holding out an exquisite cupcake with both hands, like an offering to the world.

The photos here all told stories. Maggie couldn't help but think about the photo albums at Nana's. Good photographs made everything feel so real, so close. They triggered so many memories and emotions.

"That's what baking can do," Daisy said out of nowhere. "A pastry, a loaf of good bread, a sweet bite and especially a delicious smell – the things we make in this shop are all connected to feelings and memories."

Maggie gulped. It was as if Daisy had read her thoughts.

Wait ... *Had* Daisy read her mind?

"Don't worry," Daisy said, seeming to read her mind again. "You live with your grandmother, right?"

Maggie nodded. "Yeah, Nana."

Daisy heard a change in Maggie's voice and turned from the photos on the wall to face Maggie.

"Is everything okay?"

"Not exactly," Maggie finally said. "I suppose I should tell you. My mum and dad both died. This year. In a car accident."

"Oh, Maggie," Daisy said with a little gasp.

It was the first time outside of Nana's house that Maggie had confessed the truth out loud. Usually other people around Maggie did all the explaining through whispered voices, as if it was a terrible secret that Maggie didn't already know.

"I'm so sorry," Daisy said quietly.

Maggie's stomach heaved. Why had she said anything?

"You're very brave," Daisy said. "Are you close to your Nana?"

"Yes, Nana is great," Maggie said. "She's super rich ... well, she has a big house with this nanny called Astrid, but Astrid's sort of mean. Well, I suppose she's not so mean, but she's really bossy. And my sister is so spoiled she doesn't really even think before she ..."

All at once the words came gushing out, like milk out of a jug – *glug, glug*. Maggie had been uncorked. It had been so long since she had said this much about anything. Why did she feel like talking so much now?

Daisy listened and led them to a tiny private office where she offered Maggie a seat in a large floral upholstered chair.

"I'm sorry I talked so much," Maggie said finally, after spilling all of her pent-up feelings. "But for some reason I feel like it is okay with you."

"Of course it is. We all need to talk."

"I usually just talk to my cat," Maggie admitted with a giggle that felt like some sort of release.

"Oh, you too?" Daisy smiled. "I have a cat called Sunny. She's a calico. And a *great* listener." She pointed to a framed picture of Sunny lying in the sun.

"That's so crazy!" Maggie said in surprise. "My cat is black. And I named her Moon, because she has a white spot, like the moon on a night sky."

"Moon and Sunny?" Daisy grinned. "What are the odds? Sounds like we're cosmically connected." After a thoughtful pause, she continued, "You know,

I was very close to my Nana too."

"You were?"

"Like this," Daisy said, holding up crossed fingers. "My Nana Belle inspired me to become a baker."

"She did?"

Then Daisy uncorked too. She told Maggie the whole story, or at least a part of it – how Nana Belle had made pastries and cakes forever, how one day she decided to share her recipes and cook baked goods for a local restaurant, and how she taught Daisy all of her magic baking tricks. There were so many, Daisy couldn't possibly remember them all. But she tried.

Daisy winked. "If my Nana Belle were here she'd tell you that baking is the key to life."

"No wonder I feel locked out!" Maggie laughed. "I don't know how to bake!"

"Well, let's fix that, shall we?" Daisy handed Maggie a pair of plastic gloves. "Wash your hands, put these on and then help me roll out some dough."

"What are we making?"

"You'll see. Let's get a roll on!" Daisy said with a mischievous look.

Maggie washed and slipped on the gloves and began to roll lumps of dough that were set out on a wide worktop dusted with flour. The dough was cut into cookie-sized circles. These, Daisy instructed, would be baked in a flat tin. Daisy explained each step to make mini Finnish sweetbreads, glazed with egg whites, her very own special recipe. They put in a pinch of cardamom to give the bread cake a little zip.

"Zip is the most essential ingredient," Daisy said. "And a little zip is just the thing for you right now." She winked at Maggie.

Maggie smiled, thinking back to the lime tart and the ginger cookies and Grace's "zip". Here, finally, was some zip and zing of her own.

As they worked, Daisy was still playing boss of the place, but with class. She continued to give orders and ask questions to the other bakers, while still managing to appear perfectly calm. And the action never stopped. Maggie was right in the middle of everything, powered by a flaming head of red hair tucked into a curly bun on the top of her head, Daisy-style.

While Daisy flitted around the bakery stations giving suggestions and pep talks, Maggie kept rolling and cutting. She made sixteen perfect circles. Daisy came back to help her place the rack into one of the many ovens.

"INCOMING! INCOMING!" Carlos yelled and raced into the kitchen. He waved his arms all over the place. "Got a hungry crew from the convention centre!" he announced.

Daisy smiled. "The rush is different every day," she said to Maggie. "But it's always wonderful. It's nice to be needed. You know?"

Maggie had never thought about it that way, but it was true. There were people Maggie needed – like Nana and Sofia and Daisy, and maybe even Astrid and Grace. And when Maggie thought about people who needed *her,* she thought about Grace.

While the little breads baked, Daisy got another big idea.

"Now that you've shared some of your story with me," Daisy explained, "I can show you how I really create my baked goodies. I invent every day."

Maggie grinned and looked at Daisy expectantly. It sounded like something she would like to do. Maggie pushed thoughts about messing up and making mistakes out of her mind.

Daisy pulled a lot of objects and ingredients off the shelves around them. Then she placed them onto the worktop for Maggie to see.

"Let's see. We will take some of this brown sugar ... mix in some butter ..." Daisy explained. She had a giant shaker of cinnamon in one hand and a jar of vanilla beans in the other.

Daisy heard the shop door chime as more customers came in. "Hey, Dina!" Daisy called out. "Can you take this over for me for a bit?"

"Gotcha!" Dina said, rushing over, juggling a few

different trays and pans. She eyed all the ingredients and smiled, knowingly. "I'll make the wafer cookies, no problem. You got the marshmallow filling?"

"We'll do that when we assemble," Daisy said. "Melt the chocolate too, okay?"

Somehow, without even being told *what* they were making, Dina knew.

"How do you keep track of everything?" Maggie asked, astonished.

"Magic!" Daisy said. "And teamwork," she admitted with a laugh.

Daisy took Maggie back out into the front of the bakery to help with the rush. The customers were milling around, waiting for tables to free up, while others were grabbing coffee and goodies to go. Today Daisy's Desserts was offering ten different kinds of croissant and people were buying them all: walnut raisin, raspberry, white chocolate, blueberry, cheese cream and many others.

Babs moved quickly around the seating area with a wet cloth to wipe down all those sticky tables. Carlos, who spun between the back and the front throughout the day, kept the espresso machine humming. The two part-timers helped bag, box and restock the shelves as they emptied.

"So," Daisy said, as she took money from customers, "this is how it all works around here."

"It's like a ballet, watching everyone work together. It's amazing," Maggie said.

Daisy laughed. "More of a boogie, maybe?"

When the rush was over, they headed back into the kitchen to finish up what they'd started. Dina had removed the trays from the oven and now the thin wafer cookies were cooling on the worktop.

"When we swapped stories about our cats, I got a light bulb of an idea," Daisy said. She pulled an enormous silver bowl from the rack and affixed it to a machine with a whipping whisk at its centre. Then she poured egg whites and gelatin into the bowl. The whisk began to beat furiously. Then Dina came over with a piping hot pan from the hob with a thermometer in it.

"Ready!" Dina announced.

Slowly, Daisy poured hot corn syrup into the whipped egg white mix. The mixture whirled around. Daisy added some of the vanilla and everything in the bowl stiffened.

"Marshmallow!" Maggie cried. Her eyes got big. "That's my favourite!"

"Aha! I had a suspicion! Here's what I was thinking," Daisy went on, scooping a little of the marshmallow onto a wafer cookie and then placing a second cookie on top, like a sandwich. "The perfect baked treat for *you* is something like this. All we have to do is dip it into chocolate."

Daisy took a bowl of melted chocolate that Dina had prepared. She carefully dunked the cookie sandwich into the chocolate and then rested the concoction on a large sheet of waxed paper.

"You can still see the white marshmallow on the side, right? Sort of like a white splotch, in honour of your kitty, whom you love. It's a chocolate moon!"

She handed one to Maggie. It was still a little

gooey, but Maggie took a big bite.

"*Mmmmmm,*" Maggie murmured around her mouthful.

"Hey, maybe I'll make a yellow cake and orange cream filling version of this cookie in tribute to my own cat – a Sunny Delight?" Daisy said, tapping her chin in thought. "See, baking inventions!"

Baked with love, Maggie thought as she poked her finger into the middle of her chocolate moon. "Thank you! This is officially my new favourite food!"

"Then it's 'officially' *Maggie's* Chocolate Moon!"

"Maggie's *Magic* Chocolate Moon!" Maggie corrected, waving her marshmallow-tipped finger around like a magic wand.

They assembled more of the treats, and for a brief moment, Maggie felt like she wasn't alone, like she really belonged somewhere. She imagined what Mum and Dad would say if they could see her here at the bakery, working hard and not messing up. *Could they see her?*

And she wondered what Nana and Astrid might say. She wanted to share this moment with them. Maybe she could bake these at home and impress them both? Her mind raced with plans.

"Thank *you*," Daisy said to Maggie as they put their chocolate moons into individual boxes decorated with gold foil stars.

"Thank *me*?" Maggie said. "What did I do?"

"You opened up."

Maggie took a breath. "Yeah, it felt good. I was afraid it would just make me sadder ... but it didn't."

"I knew there was something inside you needed to share. I can tell these things. Usually the stuff that's hidden away is the most important stuff."

"Like here in the bakery," Maggie said. "All the stuff behind the scenes that's hidden back here – that's where all the real stuff is going on."

"Yep. Back here is where the magic happens!" Daisy pretended to wave her own magic wand.

Maggie grabbed one of the fully assembled chocolate moons. "And now," Maggie said. "I'd like to make more magic. I, Magdalene McAllister, will make this *entire* chocolate moon disappear."

She took one ... two ... three enormous bites.

Daisy laughed and clapped loudly. "*Magnifico!*"

Chapter 6

Good things come to those who bake ...

That night Grace wouldn't stop talking about her dance class: how she was the best one in the class, how pretty she looked in her new leotard, how her teacher used to dance for some fancy-pants Russian ballet troupe. She didn't mean to be obnoxious, but that's how it came out. Maggie couldn't get a word in edgeways about her amazing afternoon at the bakery.

"I really think that if I keep dancing, I will be famous," Grace said, twirling around the room. "Like, chat-show famous!"

"What does that even mean?" Maggie asked, losing patience. She wanted to be the positive older sister. That was her job, according to Astrid and Nana. But it was hard to hang on to the wonderful, positive vibe she'd had at Daisy's. Being home with Grace and listening to her babble on and on made Maggie start to lose her grip on that little-bit-of-sugar feeling that had seemed so easy at the bakery.

"Well, I could be everyone-wants-my-autograph famous," Grace chirped.

"Wow, no self-esteem issues with you, huh?" Maggie muttered, rolling her eyes.

"I know! How about a-zillion-people-all-tweeting-about-me-on-social-media famous?" Grace said, more animated than before.

"Grace!" Maggie barked. It took all of her self-control not to come right out and thunk Grace on the head. "Would you please shut up?"

"What's the matter with *you*?" Grace said. "I know – you're jealous!"

"Hardly. Obviously you just started dancing, and in order to be famous, you have to be the very best at what you do. I just think you're getting a little ahead of yourself."

"*One day* I will be the best," Grace said with a dazzling smile. "Nana always says I can do whatever I want. Mum and Dad always said that too."

Maggie sighed. "Well, they always said that about me too. But so far I haven't become a star hockey player or the world's best flower arranger."

"You never *really* wanted to be those things," Grace said, looking sure of herself. "That's why they haven't happened."

"That's not the point!" Maggie said, exasperated, though she wasn't sure exactly what her point was.

"You're just jealous, because I know what I'm going to be when I grow up and you don't!"

"When you grow up? Grace, I'm twelve and you're nine! We have forever before we need to deal with that. And I'm sorry, but you are probably *not* going to be a top Russian ballerina."

"You're so mean!" Grace cried. "You always hurt my feelings!"

"I'm just being honest," Maggie said with a shrug.

Grace stormed out of the living room.

Oh, no. Maggie knew that was a stupid move. Before she even heard Astrid yell, she knew the badditude was back. And she was going to pay.

As expected, a moment later Astrid wailed, "MAGDALENE! I need to speak to you right now!"

Maggie needed to run somewhere – *anywhere* – or hide in her bedroom and lock the door until Astrid hunted her down. That was how it usually went. Maggie took two steps at a time up to her room, slammed the door and flung herself on her bed. The room was very quiet for a moment until she heard the thump of Astrid's footsteps. Maggie had to admit that this was not a very clever hiding spot.

Bang bang bang bang bang.

"I know you're in there," Astrid said, fist on the door. She opened it and started ranting about how Grace was so upset and how Maggie needed to think long and hard about the way she talked to her little sister and ... *Blah blah blah blah blah.*

Maggie didn't want to hear any of it. She kept as still as she could, head under her pillow. If only she were back at the bakery right now. She'd been having such a good day, and now it had all fallen apart. What had happened?

She heard Astrid give up and say, "You have a lot of thinking to do, young lady!" and then stomp back down the stairs.

Moon leaped onto the bed and purred as she rubbed her fur against Maggie's legs. She looked deep into her kitty's apricot-coloured eyes. "You understand me, don't you?" she asked the cat.

Moon just purred.

"I can't stand Grace sometimes," Maggie confessed in a seething whisper. "She thinks the world revolves around her. I always get in trouble. She's perfect. I'm not. I wish I could just go and live at Daisy's bakery and make cookies forever. Then I wouldn't have to deal with Astrid's punishments and Grace's stupid upbeat personality and all this drama ..."

Purrrrrrrrrrr.

Moon flicked her tail back and forth and it tickled Maggie's chin. She petted the cat at the very top of her soft black head and made a circle with the tip of her finger around the perimeter of Moon's white spot.

"Purrrrrr yourself," Maggie whispered more softly into Moon's ears. "You *do* understand me better than anyone." But then she thought about Daisy ... and Sofia, and she realized that maybe there were *some* people out there who understood her a little bit.

Moon flicked her tail again, like she knew *exactly* what Maggie was thinking.

What a day with Daisy – a near stranger who somehow seemed to know Maggie from the start. If Grace weren't always getting her way, Maggie would be able to spend more time at Daisy's, baking and talking and being herself like she had today. Maggie could become a real baker. She thought again of Sunday mornings in Mum's kitchen. Even though she'd never thought much about baking before, she realized she'd never felt more alive and hopeful than she had in Daisy's kitchen. Maybe those chocolate moons were another love note from Mum.

Maggie popped up off the bed and opened the laptop on her desk. She powered it up and looked for a website for Daisy's Desserts. Bingo! She found blog entries and other posts on the site. What other secrets were hidden at Daisy's?

WHERE THERE'S A WHISK, THERE'S A WAY

Learning to cook can give you a real dose of self-confidence! When you pick up a whisk or spatula, you feel ...   Read more

THERE'S A REASON THAT STRESSED IS DESSERTS SPELLED BACKWARDS

Everyone knows what it feels like to be too busy. (Well, not too busy to be reading my blog!) I like to think that a little sugar can ...   Read more

Daisy was one of the coolest people on the planet, in person and online. And she didn't just bake: she whipped and dipped and wrote all about it, and she managed to cheer people up in the process. Maggie kept reading.

I'M SUCH A DIP!

Your attention, please. I am obsessed with dipping things into chocolate. I think it started when I went to a wedding a few weeks ago. A good friend was getting married, and I provided the amazing (if I do say so myself) polka-dotted, fondant, four-tiered cake. Another friend of hers happens to be a sweet maker (second-coolest job on earth, after baker, of course!). She made chocolate-dipped tropical fruit slices. She had candied mangoes and pineapples with shredded coconut on top! Divine! Inspiration struck, and I decided to experiment in my own kitchen. Crisps (the ruffle kind hold the most chocolate!), cookies, whatever you've got – give it a shot. I officially declare today ALL THINGS MUST BE DIPPED IN CHOCOLATE DAY. If you've had the kind of day where you've acted like a dip or felt like a dip, the best cure is a chocolate dipped crisp. Guaranteed!

Maggie was enthralled by all the photographs and blog entries. What should she read next? Daisy called all of the entries her "diaries", which made perfect sense, of course. And who could resist things dipped in chocolate? Maggie continued clicking through the website. Finally she settled on page that shared the history of the bakery. There was a funny photo of Daisy in a huge pink chef hat. Maggie clicked on Daisy's bio.

Name: Daisy Jane Duncan

Home: All over with more destinations to come! One day I would love to open a bakery in Greece or maybe China. My friend once showed me how to prepare the best Cantonese dim sum. And I love making steamed egg buns with sweet custard. May need to make a version for Daisy's Desserts!

Favourite Baked Good: Doughnuts, hands down. No ... Chocolate Cheesecake recipe from Nana? No ... My own apple bars? DON'T MAKE ME CHOOSE!

Inspiration: Nana Belle. Let me tell you about my lovely Nana Belle. She is to blame for all this sugar and flour madness! When I was a little girl, she used to hum this song, "Life is Sweet", and roll out the pie dough. I remember the way her kitchen smelled, like cocoa and apple pie. Nana believed she could bake love into everything. She convinced me that I could do the same. I've seen photographs of Nana Belle when she was about my age. She had the same frizzy red hair that I do. She piled it on top of her head, just like I do. And she listened to my every word. I still believe in Nana Belle and the possibility of a good flaky crust and something chewy and fourteen kinds of cookies. I bake for her and for all of you. Nana Belle believed in baked love for all!

"A little more sugar in my life," Maggie whispered, promising herself that she'd try to be more like Daisy. She continued to click and read until a little box popped up on her screen.

It was an instant message from Sofia.

Where R U???? Let's hang out @ DD tomorrow. Can u meet? Will you be with yr sister? Byeeeee!

Maggie wanted to reply straight away, so she sent back a message saying yes, yes, YES, of course she would meet Sofia after school. She didn't have anything going on, and she hoped that Grace would have another dance class. She didn't want to drag her sister along and have her intrude on her time with Sofia. This would be her first time spending time with Sofia outside of school!

Maggie heard a timid knock on her door. *Speak of the devil,* she thought. Grace poked her head into the room. "Maggie?"

"WHAT?" Maggie snapped, already failing to implement her more "sugar" plan.

"Okay!" Grace said. "Just telling you that Astrid says you have to take me home tomorrow. Or we can go to the bakery, she said, but you have to walk me there. She has something to do."

"Are you *serious*?" Maggie moaned. It was as if Grace had sensed that Maggie had literally just made plans and instantly appeared to ruin *everything*.

"That's what Astrid said," Grace shrugged innocently.

Maggie jumped off the bed and went to find

Astrid. It wasn't fair. Maggie was making a new friend for the first time in a long time, and Grace was getting in the way. Maggie didn't want to deal with her sister.

And she definitely didn't want Grace interrupting her one-on-one time with Sofia. She could just imagine Grace taking over the conversation while Maggie would sit there in the corner like a third wheel. Was it too much to ask to just meet a friend and enjoy some freedom without having Grace in the way?

Maggie protested, but Astrid didn't want to hear any of it. She didn't care what Maggie felt. Big sisters needed to walk with little sisters, she said.

End of discussion.

"This stinks," Maggie whispered to her sister.

"Why?" Grace asked.

"You ruin everything."

"But I thought you liked our walks and talks? You said–"

"I know what I said," Maggie sighed. "Just leave me alone."

Maggie knew she was being mean, but she didn't care. The badditude was in charge once again.

Chapter 7

Not the boss of me

Friday afternoon, Maggie planned to meet Grace and Sofia in the school lobby and then they would all head to the bakery. But Grace had to stay a few minutes after school to retake a quiz, so Sofia said she'd meet them at Daisy's. She had to run a quick errand for her mum anyway.

"Come on!" Maggie said when Grace finally appeared in the lobby. Maggie was anxious to get to Daisy's and didn't want to miss any more time with Sofia.

As Maggie hurried them along the street, they passed the boutique with all the butterflies and then the dry-cleaners. Grace stopped and planted herself in front of some new shoe shop for a little while, which slowed them down.

"Come on, Grace," Maggie said, annoyed at the further delay. "Let's go."

"Hold on, I'm looking in here," Grace said. "Look at those red platforms!"

"Now you're into shoes?" Maggie said. "Keep walking!"

"Wait! No! Let me look! Just a minute! And, BTW, I'm into *everything* fashionable."

"Seriously?" Maggie yelled, looking at the time on her phone. "Grace. You're making us late! You're always saying 'just a minute' and I am so sick of that – and I'm sick of you!"

As soon as the words left her lips, Maggie knew she had been too harsh, but she just didn't feel like waiting and stopping at every single shop. She just wanted to get to Daisy's.

"You're being mean!" Grace crinkled her nose.

Maggie put her hands on her hips. "I'm not mean. *You're* selfish!"

"No, I'm not," Grace said with a pout.

"Stop pretending like you never do anything wrong," Maggie said. "You whine and complain and I'm the one who always gets blamed. It's not fair!"

"When do I blame you?" Grace said.

Maggie rolled her eyes. "You don't have to. Nana and Astrid do it for you. I get blamed for *everything*."

"Can't we just look in this shop for a minute?" Grace asked, turning back, still seeming more interested in shoes than in their argument.

Maggie threw her arms up in frustration. "This is exactly my point! You're being selfish again!"

"You are not the boss of me!" Grace stomped her foot.

Maggie huffed back in anger. "I always walk you home. Do I get thanked? No!"

Maggie could see that Grace was close to tears. But she kept going. "Whenever we get in a fight, I'm always the one who gets in trouble, because you're little miss perfect and I'm little miss ... misfit, or something!"

"What did I do wrong?" Grace sniffed.

Maggie kept going with her rant. "You waltz around like everything's great and ... everything's not great!"

"You're my big sister," Grace yelled. Now her hands were on her hips too. "You're supposed to be nice and look out for me, no matter what!"

"Well, as the big sister, I say we're leaving!" Maggie said. She turned on her heel and walked away, solo.

"No, wait! Maggie!" Grace yanked hard on Maggie's jumper and asked if they could please look in the shop, *pretty please,* just for a minute.

But Maggie had had enough. She wasn't stopping for anything.

Suddenly Sofia appeared, running across the street towards Maggie.

"Hey!" Maggie said, surprised. "I thought you'd be at Daisy's already."

"Nope, the queue at the post office was really long," Sofia said. "What's new?"

"You mean besides my annoying sister?"

"I heard that!" piped in Grace. She was following a short way behind them.

"Did you see that new boy in gym class today?" Maggie whispered to Sofia, ignoring Grace. "He landed on his head!"

"He is still cute, even with a dent in his head!" Sofia giggled.

Maggie and Sofia started chatting more about lame teachers and the bad macaroni and cheese at lunch and a boy called Luke in the class above them who got a (gasp!) purple mohawk. Other people rushed around them, but the pair didn't mind. They chatted and giggled, heads together and backpacks bumping. Grace followed behind, moping.

Serves her right, Maggie thought, *for all the times she's made* me *wait.*

Sofia's backpack buzzed. "That's my mobile phone," she said. "It might be my dad." She read the message. "Yup, he wants me to pick up some cookies while we're at Daisy's. He is like totally addicted to their Finnish sweetbread, or something like that."

"I know how to make that!" Maggie said.

"You do?" Sofia asked. "You know how to bake?" She seemed seriously impressed.

It was so nice to be with her friend instead of spending the entire walk listening to her little runt of a sister jabber on about being the top speller in Year 5 and about how many girls asked to play with her at break that day.

"Why do you think everyone likes the bakery so much?" Maggie asked, now that they were on the topic of the baking. "It's like we're all hooked on some magical ingredient."

"Yeah – sugar!" Sofia joked. "But I think it's because of the woman in charge, Daisy? She is so nice. I don't think she has any children, but she's kind of mum-like, only cooler. Well, cooler than *my* mum." Sofia laughed. "My mum is an accountant. Ugh. I wish she were a fancy baker or an actress or ..."

"A lion tamer!" Maggie smiled. "Or a scuba diver. That would be fun!"

"What does your mum do? Does she work?" Sofia asked. "Wait. She isn't an actual lion tamer, is she?" She giggled.

Maggie sighed. "Well, actually ..."

She took a deep, deep breath.

"The truth is, my parents both died in an accident ... about seven months ago," Maggie finally admitted.

Sofia gasped. "Oh! I'm so sorry."

"It's no big deal," Maggie said. "Well, it *is*, just ... don't feel bad. I haven't really wanted to talk about it."

"OMG, I didn't have a clue. Wow." Sofia glanced back and then turned around. "Wait," she said. "Wasn't your sister behind us?"

Maggie whirled around to look. "Grace?"

She didn't see her.

"Gracie? GRACE! Grace, where are you?" Maggie screeched.

"I didn't see her walk away," Sofia said. "Let's look around. I'm sure she's nearby ..."

They both called out her name. No one answered. Busy people kept rushing by, barely looking up from their phones.

Maggie panicked. "Oh no, Sofia. She must have wandered away when we were talking. Grace!"

"She probably just slipped by us and went on ahead to the bakery. Let's look."

Maggie and Sofia raced the short distance ahead and burst into Daisy's. Peering around customers, they quickly scanned the shop, eyeing the tables, looking under the displays and behind the counters.

Where had Grace gone?

"I don't see her," Sofia said, sharing her friend's worry.

Maggie got a tight knot in the deepest pit of her stomach. "I don't see her either."

"Maybe she didn't come in here," Sofia said. "Maybe she went to another shop? Let's go back and look."

They dashed back outside. Maybe Grace was just sitting on the kerb or looking in some other shop window, Maggie hoped. There were so many – *too many* – places to look.

"This is not good," Maggie said, feeling breathless. "I never should have looked away."

"I shouldn't have been distracting you," Sofia quickly said.

"No, no! It's all my fault." Maggie felt the bad kind of butterflies in her stomach.

"Let's go back and retrace our steps," Sofia said. "My mum always says to do that."

My mum always says to do that.

"I'm sorry again," Sofia said, shaking her head when she realized what she'd said.

The knot in Maggie's stomach got a little bit tighter. Maggie wished she had her own mum here right now to help her.

They retraced their steps as Sofia – or rather, Sofia's mum – had suggested. They looked on both sides of the street. They walked back by every shop they'd passed, including the shoe shop Grace had begged to look at, which was now closed. A man coming out of the dry-cleaner's nearly ran them over with an armful of clothes wrapped in plastic. The group of schoolchildren was still huddled near the doorway of Dough Boys pizzeria, shoving slices of pizza in their faces. One of the gallery owners stood outside, talking on a mobile phone.

But no Grace was in sight.

"Think, Maggie," Sofia said. "Where did Grace like to look? Was there a shop she may have gone to? Are you *sure* she didn't say something to you?"

"I don't think so," Maggie whimpered. "I can't think of where she would have gone."

"Do you think someone else picked her up?" Sofia asked.

Maggie felt a surge of emotion, but all that came out was a nervous, "Oh, no ..."

"Maybe we should tell someone she's missing," Sofia said. "This is getting kind of serious ..."

Maggie sighed shakily. She'd never felt this

much trouble on her shoulders. Nana would never forgive her if she *lost* her little sister! That was the understatement of the century.

"Maybe she left something back at school and went there?" Sofia tried new solutions.

"Maybe ... no ..." Maggie said, knowing that couldn't be it.

"I don't know. Was there some shop she really loved and might have gone to?"

"Wait! WAIT! That's it!" Maggie blurted, hugging Sofia briefly. Then she sped away. Sofia chased right behind her.

"Where are you going?" she called out. "Slow down. I'm coming!"

"I think I know where she is!" Maggie cried over her shoulder.

They weaved around people all in rushes of their own. Then Maggie brought them to a sudden halt. They were in front of Bella's Bazaar.

"She's in here," Maggie said, panting. "I know she is!"

They peered through the door and saw all the butterflies hanging from the ceiling. It looked like a light was on somewhere in the back. All those butterflies inside her stomach had pointed the way back here. Grace had to be hiding inside.

But when Maggie pulled on the door, she discovered that it was locked.

"Look," Sofia said, pointing to the sign. "The shop's closed."

Maggie looked at Sofia with fear in her eyes. "So where did Gracie go?"

"Maggie, we should tell someone. Let's go back to the bakery. We can call your mum."

"We can't call my mum!" Maggie cried, exasperated.

"I'm so sorry," Sofia covered her mouth. "I meant your grandmother. That was stupid of me." Sofia looked like she was near to tears herself.

They hurried back to the bakery, looking for Grace and calling her name the whole way. As they ran into the bakery, they nearly collided with Babs.

"Slow down, ponies!" Babs cried, chuckling. "What's all the fuss, Gus?"

"My sister!" Maggie cried, tears nearly spilling out now.

"What's the matter?" Babs said, instantly concerned.

"She's gone!" Maggie said.

"Disappeared," Sofia added.

"What? When?" Babs's jaw dropped.

"We were walking outside, and talking," Sofia explained. "And Grace was there but ... she must have wandered off."

"She was there one moment and totally gone the next!" Maggie moaned.

"Oh, my stars!" Babs whispered. "Daisy!" she called out.

Babs ushered the girls to the back of the bakery. Daisy was there with her hands full. She was working on an enormous sponge cake, clutching a tube of icing.

"D, we have a situation!" Babs declared.

"What's the matter?" Daisy put down the icing tube.

Maggie pulled herself together enough to explain whatever she could remember, how they'd been talking and then they turned around and Grace was gone. Sofia filled in other details too, like all the shops they'd revisited and all the steps they'd retraced.

Daisy furrowed her brow thoughtfully.

"I need you to both calm down," Daisy said. "Here's what we are going to do ..."

First things first: Daisy needed to call Nana to see if Grace might have gone home. Watching Daisy dial made Maggie as nervous as a cat. Nana would explode with worry. Nearly twenty minutes had already passed from the time Maggie last saw her sister.

They had to act fast.

Maggie gave her the number. Daisy called, and Maggie heard Astrid pick up. She could hear Astrid's voice shouting through the receiver ... from the opposite side of the room. Grace wasn't at home.

"Okay, so your Nana is on the way over to the bakery," Daisy said calmly, after she'd hung up.

Maggie gulped. "She is?"

"I have one more call to make," Daisy said as she began dialling again. She rang up the local police station to ask for one of the officers to come by the bakery. Maggie wondered if it was really necessary to get police involved; it was too scary to think about how serious this actually was if police were coming. But Daisy insisted.

"Better safe than sorry." She patted Maggie's hair. "That's what they all say."

Then Daisy really whirled into action. She asked more questions of Maggie.

"What does your sister usually do when you walk home?"

"She always jumps around a little, but she never goes too far," Maggie answered, searching her mind for clues.

Daisy said with a soft smile, "We're going to find her. You need to stay strong, okay?"

The police officer greeted Daisy quickly when he arrived at the bakery. Everyone moved to one of the outside tables. The officer asked even more questions that made Maggie's head spin.

"What kinds of shops did Grace like to look at?"

"Where did she like to go best?"

"Was she allowed to cross the street by herself?"

"Might she have gone back to school?"

"Did she maybe run into one of her own friends?"

Sofia put her hand around Maggie's shoulder. "We'll find her soon," she whispered. "She probably just got mixed up."

"But what if she didn't? What if someone kidnapped her? What if she got on a bus – or *hit* by a bus?" Maggie started to imagine all the worst possible things. "Oh, Sofia. This is bad."

Maggie's pulse pounded. She knew Grace couldn't have gone very far. Or had she? How long had Maggie and Sofia been talking? Was Grace so angry at Maggie that she would have tried to run away?

All the details of the afternoon were mixed up inside Maggie's brain.

And what if something *really* bad *had* happened to Grace?

Her heart sank.

She'd already lost her mum and dad. Maggie couldn't stand to lose anyone else.

Chapter 8

Saving Grace

Everyone reorganized to go on a wider search of the area.

Maggie thought hard. There had to be some clue right in front of her nose that she was missing. *Something*! If only Moon, her lucky kitty, were nearby. Moon would know the way to Grace.

"Wait!" Maggie's eyes got wide. "A whole section on kitties!"

Everyone looked at her like she was crazy, but all at once Maggie had remembered something she hadn't yet told Babs or Daisy or the police officer.

"What is it, sweetheart?" the officer asked.

"The bookshop! I think maybe Grace went inside there!" Maggie cried. "She has been talking about this one book she wants to get. And we were near there today, and she and I sort of had a fight ..."

"A fight?" the police officer interrupted.

"Well, we were mad. It wasn't that bad. I just kept walking. I thought she was behind me."

"Yes!" Sofia chimed in. "The bookshop *has* to be it. The one that's off on that side street? We didn't think to look there when we went down the street before."

Just then Nana's limo pulled up and screeched to a halt.

Astrid was out first and held the door for Nana, who wobbled a little as she rushed to get out. Maggie went right over, encouraged by her new bookshop theory.

But there was Astrid, arms crossed with disapproval.

Maggie fell into Nana's arms. "I am so sorry," Maggie said. "I'm so sorry! I was walking and we were together but then ..."

"Calm down, dear," Nana said, stroking Maggie's head.

"Nana, I think I know where she is now!" Maggie said, pulling away,

"You *think*?" Astrid huffed. "Officer, what's going on?"

No one came right out and *blamed* Maggie for what had happened, but Maggie thought that that's what everyone was thinking. In their eyes, and in her own, she was always messing up. Grace, as usual, was blameless.

Maggie knew this was going to get worse before it got better – at least worse for her. If they found Grace, Maggie would get into trouble. If they didn't ... well, Maggie couldn't bear to think about that.

"Officer, I'm the missing girl's grandmother," Nana told the police officer as they hurried in the direction of the bookshop. Astrid marched behind them.

Everyone moved quickly down the street and around the corner to the bookshop. The entourage was a small pack of curiosity seekers mixed in with Maggie's family, Daisy's entire bakery staff and several of her customers.

Mr Weller leaned in his doorway under a great big awning. He looked very confused at the crowd that approached with a police officer in the lead.

"Uh, can I help you?" he asked everyone at once, nervously pulling on his beard.

"We have a missing child," the officer said.

"Oh my!" Mr. Weller said.

Maggie pushed her way to the front. There was no time for small talk. She knew this place was one enormous pile of books with hundreds of shelves crammed in together like Jenga blocks. Who could find anything – or anyone – in here? Especially someone as small as Grace? Maggie bellowed through the door in her loudest voice possible.

"*GRAAAAACE!*"

"Is this shop up to code?" the officer asked Mr Weller, looking up at the towering bookshelves with concern.

Mr Weller nodded. "Absolutely. We have plenty

of code books ..."

Maggie had a hunch. She pushed her way into the centre of the shop.

"GRACIE!" she cried out again, even louder this time. Soon the others in the group followed her inside, shouting Grace's name too.

That's when Maggie heard a knocking. It was soft, barely audible. Then she heard a muffled yell too. Was that ... *Grace?*

"Over here!" Maggie called out to the others.

Sofia, Nana, Astrid, Daisy and the officer came over to where Maggie was standing.

"What's inside there?" Maggie asked Mr Weller, pulling at the handle of the door.

"Storage. An old sofa ..."

"Hey is someone out there?" a muffled voice cried again. "This door won't open!"

Grace!

Mr Weller's eyes grew wide. "That door sticks!" he cried and quickly began pulling on the handle. The police officer helped un-wedge the door from its stuck position, and finally it opened.

Grace was inside, unharmed, with dozens of books on kittens and fashion splayed open on a tattered sofa behind her.

Nana let out a relieved gasp. "Grace Elizabeth!"

"Nana? What are you doing here? And Astrid? Where's Maggie?"

"You had us scared silly," Astrid said.

Nana threw her arms around Grace.

"I found some books and then saw this cozy reading room. I didn't know the door was stuck shut until just now, when I heard all the shouting. There's so many cool books in here!"

"You walked away!" Maggie yelled, coming out from behind Mr Weller. "You scared me!"

"You didn't hear me say I wanted to stop and look at that one book?" Grace asked meekly.

And all at once, Maggie felt that tidal wave coming up. Only this time, nothing was holding it back. She sobbed, and the tears came flowing out.

For the first time in a long time, Maggie

really cried.

"Now, now, all's well that ends well," Nana said, patting Maggie on her back. Then Nana turned and vigorously shook hands with everyone who'd helped to find her granddaughter.

Maggie kept sobbing and waited for Astrid or Nana to scold Grace for having wandered off. But the scolding never came. Maggie couldn't believe that Grace didn't get into trouble – not even the teeniest bit – after what she'd done. Typical!

Mr Weller apologized to Nana, Astrid and the others about the mishap. He promised to get the latches fixed so no one else would get stuck inside. Still, the police officer wrote him a ticket for breaking fire code or something like that. Nana said she'd even pay to fix the door. No one seemed mad at all – except Maggie.

As they walked over to the limousine, Astrid whispered. "Wipe your face, Magdalene."

Maggie wiped. Her nose was running now too.

Her eyes were probably puffy pink from all the tears.

Suddenly Daisy appeared next to Maggie. "You going to be okay?" she asked. "You didn't do anything wrong, Maggie. In fact, you did everything right. *You* found her."

"I'm so embarrassed," Maggie said, giving her a weak smile. "I never cry."

Then Sofia appeared on Maggie's other side. She laughed. "Everyone cries, Maggie!"

"Even me," Daisy said, wiping a tear from the corner of her eye with a tissue.

Nana had rolled down the limousine window. "Hop in, dear," she said to Maggie. "Thank you, Daisy, for all your help. We'll certainly be back to the bakery soon. We won't get lost along the way, will we, children?"

Daisy agreed. "Yes, no getting lost. And I better get back to my kitchen!"

"I better get going too," Sofia said, then added, "See? I told you being friends with you would be interesting!" She gave Maggie a quick hug before she hurried off down the street.

Maggie-nificent!

For the next few days, things were pretty quiet. School was going okay. Maggie still sat with Sofia and the other girls, though still at the end of the table. Sofia insisted on calling Maggie "Super Mags", because she said Maggie was a superhero for finding Grace. Maggie was grateful for Sofia, who made things so much better than they used to be.

Things will keep getting better, Maggie told herself. She knew she needed to be patient. Nana was always telling her "patience is a virtue" and "change takes time". Every time Maggie checked Daisy's baking blog there was some new, inspiring post about baking and life – and *baked love.*

One night, Maggie went to bed a little bit earlier than usual. The house was quiet except for the low rumble of the radiators and the distant hum of Nana's television. Maggie threw herself across her puffy quilt and gazed out at the darkening sky.

There was something oddly magical and exciting about heading to bed on the early side. She mostly did it when she had a fever or when she'd been sent up to her room without dessert. (Astrid and Nana had actually enforced that punishment twice when Maggie's badditude made her say something especially rude.)

Stars were often hard to see because of the haze of city lights in the sky, but Maggie saw one bright, round object shining boldly above the buildings across the street.

"Do you see that?" Maggie asked her cat, pointing up at the shimmering moon.

Moon purred.

"Maybe that's Mum and Dad up there," Maggie said.

Her bedroom door creaked open. The hall light poured into her room. "Can I come in?" Grace asked timidly.

"You already are in."

Grace crept over to the bed.

"What's the matter now?" Maggie asked.

"Can't sleep."

"Me neither. Look at the sky with me."

"Wow," Grace said. "I can't see any of this sparkly stuff from my window."

"Yeah. Look at that moon." They lay there in silence, watching.

"I see the moon and the moon sees me ..." Grace finally whispered.

Maggie felt her chest heave.

She leaned over and wrapped her arms around her little sister. "You drive me really, really crazy, you know that?" she said.

"What?" Grace cried.

Maggie squeezed even tighter. "You scared me. I was so, so, SO scared when you got lost, Gracie."

Grace gave her a quizzical look, not sure what Maggie was saying.

"You drive me crazy, but I love you more than anything, you dummy," Maggie said, touching her forehead to her sister's.

"You do?"

"To the moon and back!" Maggie said. "All the way to Mum and Dad."

The cat, hearing her name and feeling quite left out of the hug-fest, jumped on top of both girls and began to press her paws into their heads. The sisters burst into giggles.

"What's all this racket?" a voice boomed.

The light in the bedroom clicked on. There stood Astrid in her ready-for-bed housecoat, hair down like a witch's, mug of tea in one hand. She looked very confused. One look at dear old Astrid and the giggling began all over again.

"I was just going to bed and I thought you two were at it, fighting again, but I see that I was wrong. Is everything all right?"

"Everything is hunky dory," Grace said in a goofy voice.

Maggie poked her.

"OW!" Grace cried and then giggled some more.

"Why, may I ask, is the cat on your heads?" Astrid asked.

More giggles.

"We were just looking at the moon," Maggie said.

"With Moon!" Grace added as the cat flicked her tail in Grace's eyes.

Bigger giggles.

Astrid was so silent that Maggie got a nervous pang in her gut. This moment had been perfect, one of the first perfect moments since before the accident, really. She was afraid of Astrid taking it away and expected her to bark some kind of order like, "Get back to your room right now, young lady!" Or perhaps, "I don't like this funny business during bedtime, girls!"

But instead, Astrid, who rarely smiled, *smiled*. Then she clicked off the light.

"Well, goodnight, you two gigglers," Astrid said. And then she was gone.

Maggie listened close as Astrid's footsteps got softer and softer. Then the girls were alone again. Well, *almost.*

After all, Mum, Dad and the moon were looking down upon them both.

The next day, Maggie got a great big, wonderful, chocolatey idea.

She asked Nana if she could go to the supermarket. She needed to purchase some ingredients for a very special treat. Maggie wanted to make something special for Nana and Grace, for Mum and Dad, and for Moon too! And even for Astrid. Astrid was family too, in a way. Maggie wanted to show them that she was in the middle of things – not at the end of the table.

Of course Astrid insisted on coming with Maggie to the shop. She said she had some things to get too, but Maggie assumed that Astrid just wanted to keep an eye on her. Maggie moved quickly through the aisles while Astrid pushed the cart. Maggie kept checking her list so she wouldn't forget any of the ingredients from the new recipe Daisy had given her.

"What are you making anyway?" Astrid asked in her usual bossy tone of voice.

"It's a surprise. For everyone," Maggie said.

"Maggie, I must say–" Astrid began, and Maggie waited for the lecture. But instead, Astrid said, "Your Nana is very proud of you. And so am I. And I know your mother would be too." Her voice broke just a bit. "You've shown great maturity recently."

Maggie stared at Astrid in shock.

"Of course, I still need to supervise your use of the oven," Astrid continued. And then she winked.

But when they got home, Astrid got distracted by housework. So she left Maggie in the kitchen with the cat, a basket filled with ingredients and the hot oven – unsupervised. Nana was in the other room painting with Grace. Maggie felt a sense of victory.

After about an hour, Astrid swept into the kitchen. She couldn't believe her eyes.

"There's no mess," she said with disbelief.

Maggie nodded proudly. "Daisy taught me how to keep my worktop clean while I bake," she said.

"Oh," Astrid said, impressed. "And what's over there, under that towel?"

"Get Nana and Grace, please?" Maggie said. "My surprise is ready."

Everyone went into the conservatory. Maggie told them that she wanted the sunlight to be bright and everyone to be happy.

She carried in a tray with her surprise: a fresh-baked batch of Maggie's Magic Chocolate Moons.

Nana and Astrid oohed. "You made these all by yourself?" Grace asked.

"I even made my own marshmallow."

"You learned from that baker woman Daisy, didn't you?" Nana asked. "She's a marvel, that one!"

Maggie nodded. "Take a bite! Take a bite!"

Everyone, of course (especially Grace) ate up

the chocolate treat as quickly as they could. Nana even decided to have a second one, she loved them so much.

In that moment Maggie realized that baked love was a real thing. Daisy's Desserts brought her back into a good place at home.

"Chocolate Moons are perfect!" Grace declared. She broke off a little piece for Moon the cat, but she was way too finicky. She went right for Grace's glass of cold milk instead.

"*Maggie's* Chocolate Moons are perfect," Nana agreed, licking her lips and reaching out to squeeze Maggie's hand.

Then Maggie looked to Astrid for her approval. She knew it didn't matter, not really, if Astrid liked them or not. It wasn't her job to be sweet and nice. It was her job to be in charge.

But still.

Astrid had a funny look on her face as she ate, and for a moment Maggie expected her to make some critical comment, about how the cookies were too fattening or that the chocolate was *too* sweet for her.

But Astrid didn't say either of those things. In fact, she didn't say anything. She ate her cookie down to the very last crumb and then stood up and pulled Maggie out of her chair.

Oh no, Maggie thought. *Now here's the lecture.*

But then Astrid hugged Maggie – hard. "It has been a long, tough year, hasn't it, Magdalene?" Astrid said. "I hope I didn't make it harder. I thought I was helping … but maybe not in the right way."

Maggie didn't know what to say to that. So she said the only thing that made any sense. "Have another chocolate moon?" she asked "They make everything better."

"No," Astrid said. "*You* make everything better."

"Now, now, you'll make me cry!" Nana chimed in.

Grace bounced out of her seat, excited. "Wait! I know! I know!"

"What, Grace?" Maggie groaned, expecting Grace to somehow steal the spotlight.

"I know why the chocolate moons are magical."

"Huh?" Maggie asked. "Why?"

Grace made a funny face. "Because when Maggie was baking them, she said the magic word."

"What's that, dear?" Nana asked.

"Maggie-nificent!"

Everyone laughed together, even Astrid. And it was a magical, marshmallow moment, indeed. Even if Moon (the one with fur) didn't want anything to do with that treat.

Back to the blog

Home
Meet the bakers
Recipes
- Cakes
- Cookies
- Tray bakes
- Breads
- Gluten free
- Vegan
- Dairy free
- Other

Archive
- January
- February
- March

Dear Sweeties,

Baked love is very real. Take a listen and notice how often you hear someone say "Hey, Honey!" or "She's a real sweetie!" Terms of endearment often start with sugar, and for good reason.

Sometimes life gives us lemons, and all we can do is add sugar and try to make lemonade ... or lemon meringue pie ... or lemon pound cake ... or lemon crepes ... or, well, you get the idea! We do whatever we can to take the sour away.

On that note, I want to say here how much I love you all. Some of you sit under my lollipop chandelier in the shadows of the cakes and cookies and do your homework or draw fabulous pictures or just dream. Others come to me for a little sugar – when everything seems decidedly un sweetened in life. I notice you, all of you, whether you're ringing the bell for service or sitting quietly in the corner.

I promise – there's always a treat waiting here for you.

See you in the kitchen!

xo, Daisy

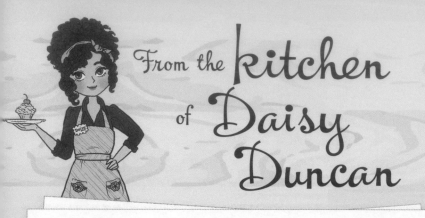

From the kitchen of Daisy Duncan

Maggie's magic chocolate moons

With this shortcut version of Daisy's recipe, you can make chocolate "moons" like Maggie did in the story. Just make sure you ask an adult for help when you use equipment in the kitchen. Daisy would want you to be extra careful!

Ingredients:

one pack round chocolate
    wafer cookies (any brand)
baking sheet
220 grams marshmallow
    topping

Directions:

1. Line up half the cookies on baking sheet with flat side up.

2. Spoon the marshmallow topping into a bowl and microwave for 15 seconds.

3. Spread a thin layer of marshmallow on flat side of each cookie and top with second cookie like a sandwich.

4. Dot each sandwich with more marshmallow topping, so it looks like a moon cookie!

Bonus: If you're not in the mood for super-sticky, you can put whipped cream between your cookies instead!

Meet the bakers

Daisy

Owner of Daisy's Desserts! With a frizzy head of magical red hair, sunny disposition and a treasure trove of recipes passed down from her dear Nana Belle, this always-optimistic baker is ready to serve you! Along with her crazy baking team – Dina, Babs and Carlos – Daisy aims to transform our city neighbourhood with sugar, spice and everything nice. From custard tarts to cupcakes, Daisy always seems to have the recipe for "baked love" up her flour-dusted sleeve. Inside Daisy's Desserts, the impossible somehow becomes iced with possibility!

Dina

Baker and waitress Dina specializes in sweets, especially when it comes to her personality! Designated mother hen of the crew, Dina not only has a way with a rolling pin and a whisk but also with our customers! She is always suggesting new recipes and encouraging Daisy to try new ingredients from around the globe.

Carlos

Daisy's number-one confidante and trusted sidekick in the kitchen, Carlos has a twinkle in his eye and pep in his step. A family man with four sweet-toothed children at home, Carlos is always inventing and testing new recipes in the kitchen of Daisy's Desserts. He is the master mix-man: to date, he's invented cookies, cakes and even Daisy's line of sweet treats for dogs. His favourite saying is, "I keep experimenting until I find the right formula!"

Babs

Like a Hollywood starlet from another era, Babs is always dressed to impress with a bouffant do and an apron to match every shade of lipstick. Our wisecracking baking beauty has a lingo all her own, calling customers "peach" or "sugar" before sneaking them samples of Daisy's latest baked goodies. Babs is also our bakery's guardian angel: years ago, she was BFFs with Daisy's Nana Belle.

Talk it out with Daisy!

Little sisters can be really annoying – just ask Maggie!

How does Maggie's relationship with Grace change over the course of the story?

If Maggie were your friend, what advice would you give her?

If you have siblings, can you relate to Maggie's frustrations?

Good friends can help you through life's challenges. Come up with some examples in the story where you see evidence of good friendships. Then think of a time in your life when you were a good friend or someone was a good friend to you.

Laura Dower

About the author

Laura Dower worked in marketing and editorial in children's publishing for many years before taking a big leap to the job of full-time author. She has published more than 100 children's books, including the popular tween series *From the Files of Madison Finn*. A longtime Girl Scout leader and Cub Scout leader, Laura lives with her family in New York, USA.

Lilly Lazuli

About the illustrator

London based illustrator Lilly Lazuli has a penchant for all things colourful and sweet! Originally from Hawaii, Lilly creates artwork that has a bright and cheerful aesthetic. She gains most of her inspiration from travelling, vintage fashion and ogling beautiful cakes. She enjoys making eye-catching artwork that makes people smile.

For MORE GREAT BOOKS go to

www.raintree.co.uk